'Well?' Gabr **which was a** **position beca** **her eye level a** **comfort.**

Rose could so easily slide her hand under his silk robe. Years' worth of fantasies crashed through her like a tidal wave, and she closed her eyes briefly.

She opened them to find that he was even closer to her. And amused. And here she was, desperately trying to fight down the effect he was having on her. Four years fighting off a lethal attraction to a man who had now decided that it might be a bit of fun to flirt with her once in a while.

'If you hadn't been flirting with me,' Rose said. 'If you hadn't forgotten that it's totally inappropriate. I expected more of you.'

She had been hoping to shame him. She failed. He gave her a slow, devastating smile.

'Flirting…' He inclined his head to one side, as if considering a new-found concept. 'You're right. Maybe flirting was a bad idea. Maybe…' his voice was velvety soft and rich with husky sexuality '…I should have just done this…'

Cathy Williams is originally from Trinidad, but has lived in England for a number of years. She currently has a house in Warwickshire, which she shares with her husband Richard, her three daughters, Charlotte, Olivia and Emma, and their pet cat, Salem. She adores writing romantic fiction and would love one of her girls to become a writer—although at the moment she is happy enough if they do their homework and agree not to bicker with one another.

Recent titles by the same author:

AT THE GREEK TYCOON'S PLEASURE
AT THE GREEK TYCOON'S BIDDING
THE ITALIAN'S PREGNANT MISTRESS

THE ITALIAN BOSS'S SECRETARY MISTRESS

BY
CATHY WILLIAMS

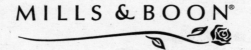

All the characters in this book have no existence outside the imagination of the author, and have no relation whatsoever to anyone bearing the same name or names. They are not even distantly inspired by any individual known or unknown to the author, and all the incidents are pure invention.

First published in Great Britain 2006
Paperback edition 2007
Harlequin Mills & Boon Limited,
Eton House, 18-24 Paradise Road, Richmond, Surrey TW9 1SR

© Cathy Williams 2006

ISBN-13: 978 0 263 85296 7
ISBN-10: 0-263-85296-2

Set in Times Roman 10½ on 12¾ pt
01-0207-53346

Printed and bound in Spain
by Litografia Rosés, S.A., Barcelona

THE ITALIAN BOSS'S SECRETARY MISTRESS

CHAPTER ONE

IT WAS not yet seven-thirty and Gabriel Gessi was already at his desk. It was his daily routine. Half an hour running on the treadmill at his gym, half an hour scything through the empty pool, a quick shower, a shave and then on to his office, already charged to face the onslaught that constituted his average day. The only interruptions to this brutally physical routine came in the form of his frequent trips overseas, although, even then, he would try his level best to kick-start his working day on a physical high.

The past three months had not seen him deviate from this punishing routine, even though the accustomed high had been marred by a succession of irritations that he really should not have been expected to handle. Even though they concerned him.

Gabriel Gessi inhabited that rarefied world of the supremely wealthy and, as such, was not accustomed to dealing with life's minor irritations. His adrenalin rush came from the aggressive cut and thrust of deals and acquisitions, not from the more prosaic set-backs that dogged most people's working lives.

Set-back number one had come in the form of the temp who had sailed through the interview process under the successful camouflage of an efficient working girl but who, after one week, had turned out to be a ditzy emotional wreck who spent the majority of her two weeks sniffing discreetly into a handker-chief and muttering lame excuses about boyfriend problems.

Gabriel had no time for females with boyfriend problems and even less time for females who cried. He had had to get rid of her and thereafter had followed a catalogue of mediocrity which had left him gritting his perfect white teeth in frustration.

He couldn't imagine how the incompetents who appeared in front of him could ever have been fortunate enough to find gainful employment and yet, by all accounts, they had.

He had seen off the last one the Friday before with an audible sigh of relief. She, at any rate, had lasted longer than the expected fortnight, but he reckoned that that had only been because he had swallowed his irritation and, with laudable patience, tolerated her annoying tendency to cower whenever he spoke and to address him so quietly that he'd constantly had to tell her to speak up. Whenever he'd told her to speak up, she'd invariably jumped and spilled something. Coffee. Water. Her cup of tea. Something of a liquid nature had always seemed to be around waiting to be nudged accidentally over, which, in turn, had rendered her even more incapable.

The whole thing had been extremely trying and Gabriel was overjoyed that his life was now going to return to normal.

For the first time in three long months, he had actually strolled through the smoked glass doors of his very plush four-storied offices without a scowl on his face.

Rose would be back today. Life could return to its normal smooth course, leaving him to get on with the process of running an empire without having to worry about the tiresome nuts and bolts.

Of course it was not yet eight and, even though he half expected her to demonstrate her enthusiasm to be back at the helm, he did not reasonably expect her to appear, like him, at the crack of dawn. She would, after all, probably still be re-cuperating from jet lag. A flight back from Australia was enough to throw even the most seasoned traveller, and Rose was not a seasoned traveller. Even though a fair percentage of his business was founded on the leisure industry, includ-ing a range of exclusive hotels scattered all over the world, her knowledge of foreign shores was limited. In the four years she had worked for him, she had only travelled with him a handful of times and, even then, only to Europe. He hadn't minded. He needed her back at the office anyway, in his absence, making sure that things were ticking over.

In that quiet time before employees started arriving, time which he usually spent going through the emails which would have been forwarded overnight, Gabriel instead swivelled his leather chair round so that he was facing the huge window, staring out at a skyline that was cluttered with the busyness of the concrete jungle, but still oddly beautiful against the crisply blue May sky.

The past three months had showed him how much he relied on Rose. She was well paid but he contemplated giving her another pay rise. Or maybe a company car, although he couldn't imagine her driving to work. Who did? He, person-ally, either took a cab or else was driven in by his chauffeur, sparing him the horrors of the London traffic. But she might be able to use a car if she ever wanted to get out of London.

Briefly, Gabriel wondered whether she ever did. Despite his occasional prodding, he realised that he knew precious little about her personal life. She had a talent for deflecting unwanted questions that would have guaranteed her a career in the diplomatic service.

Did she even have a driving licence? He vaguely assumed that everyone did, but maybe not.

Wrapped up in the lazy perambulations of his thoughts, he was only marginally aware of time passing and not at all aware that it was nine until, reflected in the glass pane through which he was still staring, he saw her standing in the open doorway that separated his office from her working area.

For a few seconds he was aware of an unusual slam of emotion, then he glanced at his watch and swivelled round.

Rose involuntarily drew in a deep breath, releasing it very slowly. It steadied her nerves. Even when she had been coming in every day, seeing him every day, he still had, had he but known it, an oddly destabilising effect on her. Something about his sheer, overpowering physicality.

Three months spent away intensified the effect to the point that she felt faint, even though her face remained as pleasantly unrevealing as always.

'It's nine o'clock,' Gabriel said, scowling. 'You normally get in by eight-thirty.'

The brusqueness of his tone released her from her immobility and she walked towards the chair positioned in front of his desk and sat down. 'I see you haven't changed, Gabriel,' she commented dryly. 'Still avoiding all the rules of common politeness. Aren't you going to ask me about my trip to Australia?'

'No need. I gathered from your emails that you were having a whale of a time. You've changed. You've lost weight.'

Rose couldn't help it. She blushed as his blue eyes gave her the once-over.

She fought to remember what her sister had said about getting out of the rut she was in, tearing herself away from her hopeless infatuation with a man who was a health hazard when it came to members of the opposite sex.

But he was just so sinfully sexy. It was impossible not to

feel her toes curl in her sensible flats as she drank in the sensuous curve of his mouth, the powerful beauty of his features, the daunting perfection of his body.

'Yes, I have,' she admitted steadily, looking down at the letter on her lap and nervously smoothing her fingers over it. 'It was hot over there. I lived on salads. I'm sorry you had such a problem with my replacements,' she said, changing the subject because those amazing eyes of his were boring holes through her. 'I honestly thought that Claire was going to work out or else I wouldn't have recruited her. What exactly was the problem?'

Gabriel, however, was still reeling from the transformation, not sure that he liked what he was seeing. Gone was the comfortably plump Rose, last seen in a practical navy-blue suit and white roll-neck sweater. In its place was a very slim Rose, showing off a surprisingly eye-catching figure in a tan and black checked skirt that actually revealed a bit of thigh and a figure-hugging black three-quarter length T-shirt that revealed breasts that would be more than just a good handful. The only sensible thing about her were her flat ballet style shoes.

'I never knew you had legs,' he mused aloud.

'Of course I have legs, Gabriel! How do you think I manage to get from A to B? On wings?'

'But you've always hidden them before...' He moved swiftly from chair to desk and perched there, staring down at her assessingly. 'And very attractive they are, too. But you might want to observe a little more decorum in the office.'

Rose's mouth dropped open in outrage at his openly sexist remark.

'What have you done to your hair? Have you done something to your hair? It looks different.'

'I haven't *done anything* to my hair, Gabriel, aside from

having it trimmed, and shall we leave the subject of me behind just for a moment...?' She fiddled with the letter, not quite knowing how she was going to give it to him without having to sit through the torturous process of watching him read it.

'Why? I'm fascinated by the transformation. I thought you were going over to help your sister with her new baby. I had no idea you were going for a complete make-over.'

'I *did* go to help Grace!'

'And in the process decided to go on a crash diet, cut your hair and lounge around in a bikini all day so that you could go brown...?'

Rose counted to ten and wondered what exactly she saw in a man who was as arrogant as they came and saw nothing amiss in barging through every warning red light she was giving off without a second's thought.

'Have you ever been in the company of a newborn, Gabriel?'

'Now that's something I've always tried to avoid...'

'Thought so, because if you had you would know that screaming newborns and tanning on loungers are two things that don't go hand in hand.'

'Surely your sister didn't expect you to look after the thing the whole time!'

'It wasn't a thing. It was a baby. A beautiful little boy. They called him Ben.' Her voice softened as she remembered the feel of that small, wriggling, plump body in her arms, a sensation that had kick-started her determination to change the rut into which she had comfortably sunk. Grace, two years older than her, had been so blissfully happy. Next to her, Rose had had an ugly vision of her own life and its sad limitations and she hadn't cared for what she had glimpsed. In two years' time she would be twenty-eight, the same age as her sister, but would she be cradling a newborn infant with a loving husband by her side if she continued doing what she was doing—working flat out for a man who didn't have a clue she existed aside from her role as his capable secretary? Or would she be the eternal career girl who spent her life improving her house and bettering her lifestyle with nothing to show for it in the end? Well, nothing worth having, anyway. A certain wistfulness crept into her voice as she told him about her experiences in Australia. Grace's husband, Tom, was an orthopaedic surgeon and had needed his nights to be free of interruption so that he could get enough sleep to enable him to operate safely. Hence, Rose's input had been more than just a luxury. She had done her fair share of waking up during the nights, settling the baby back to sleep after his feed, but she had enjoyed every minute of it.

Gabriel was hardly listening to her spiel about the baby. Babies would doubtless eventually come for him—he was, after all, half Italian—but for the moment he couldn't care less about the antics of some undersized human being on the other side of the world.

He was far too engrossed in the nut-brown creature sitting in front of him. The nut-brown creature with the abundant breasts, to which his eyes were repeatedly drawn.

At the risk of appearing pathetically lecherous and feeling an unwelcome stirring in his loins, Gabriel removed himself back to his chair and tried to focus on what she was saying about baby Ben and the crazy inaccuracy of his baby clock. He had never seen that soft look in her eyes before, and he suddenly frowned.

'I hope this trip hasn't put ideas into your head,' he said, interrupting her in mid-sentence, and Rose blinked.

'Sorry?'

'Trip? Ideas? Your head?'

'I don't know what you're talking about,' Rose told him bluntly.

'I'm talking about my perfect secretary suddenly deciding that the time has come for her to dip her toes into motherhood. All that baby business can prove contagious sometimes. I know that for a fact.'

'Oh, really, Gabriel…' Rose felt a cold anger sweep through her and she had to make a big effort to keep her voice level. 'And how would you know that?'

'I have two sisters and a brother and both my sisters have children, roughly the same ages. I have it on good authority that other women are often afflicted by maternal feelings the minute they get too close to a newborn baby…'

Rose looked at that dangerously sexy face and was unsurprised at his dismissive tone when referring to babies, parenthood and all that that implied. He was a man to whom settling down would be a notion best left on the back burner for as long as was humanly possible. Why complicate a perfectly satisfactory life, having any woman at the click of a finger, by choosing one woman and then, to compound the error, having a child? A screaming, demanding infant that would put paid to all thoughts of mobility?

'I don't intend to be trying motherhood any time soon,' Rose said coolly. 'I believe it's necessary to have a serious partner before a woman takes a step like that.'

In that one sentence Gabriel had more insight into Rose than he had ever had. He had always assumed that there was no man on the scene but only because she had never mentioned one and women generally couldn't help mentioning the men in their lives. Now it was confirmed and he was quietly pleased.

'And there's no man in your life at the moment?' he risked,

pressing on in the face of her obvious reluctance to prolong the subject.

Rose flushed and wanted to kick herself for the revealing crack in her armour. She had managed to keep their relationship on a strictly business level by making sure never to reveal anything about herself. She had instinctively known that the more he knew about her, the more dangerous her silly infatuation with him became. He could charm the birds from the trees and without really trying he could easily have sussed how she felt about him had he known anything about her private thoughts.

Of course it no longer mattered. She was forgetting that in the heat of the moment. The realisation gave her the strength she needed and she smiled nonchalantly.

'They come and go,' she said airily. 'You know how it is. I'm between chaps at the moment.' The small white lie was worth every penny just to see the incredulity in his eyes and she smiled demurely, daring him to voice his shock that she might actually have a life outside his corporation. 'Anyway…' she fingered the letter nervously '…now that I've told you all about my trip to Australia, there's something I need to give you…' She stretched forward and placed the white envelope on his desk and a sudden rush of sickening nerves flooded through her in a tidal sweep.

But she reminded herself that she was absolutely doing the right thing. She had talked it over with Grace and just voicing her thoughts had been sufficient to make her realise what she needed to do, how badly she needed to escape the powerful net Gabriel had spread around her over the years to the point where he was always somewhere in her head, whatever the time of day or night, whoever she might or might not be with. It was dangerous and getting more so with each passing day. In another four years' time her emotions would be so tethered to him that she might well find herself crippled by her own inability to find a suitable mate without resorting to unfavourable comparisons.

He was looking at the letter warily, but he eventually took it, ripped it open and quickly scanned the contents. Several times. Obviously thinking that he had misread something. Finally, when her nerves were on the point of totally shredding, he said, very softly, 'What's going on here, Rose?' Shock and disbelief flared in his deep blue eyes and Rose automatically cringed back, her normal assertive crispness abandoning her in the face of his concentrated, focused energy.

'It's my letter...of...of resignation...'

'I know *what it is!* I can read perfectly well! What I *don't understand* is why it's staring me in the face!' The pleasant anticipation with which his day had optimistically dawned, when he had contemplated the satisfaction of his life being returned to normal, now seemed like a distant thing of the past.

First of all, she had strolled in way later than she normally would have, sporting a changed look that would have had every man's head reeling in appreciation as she strode through the office and, as if that hadn't been bad enough, she had flung a resignation note down on his desk with all the preliminaries of someone who could not give a damn.

Gabriel, in addition to feeling rage and bewilderment, was assailed by a sense of bitter betrayal.

'I just feel...'

'I mean, *no warning!*' he said, interrupting her harshly, waving the sheet of paper about in an accusatory fashion. 'You stroll in here at God only knows what time...'

'Eight-forty-five!' Rose objected. 'Fifteen minutes before I'm technically due to start the working day!'

Gabriel chose to ignore her input. 'And suddenly you're telling me that you're walking out on me!'

'I'm not *walking out on you*.' Rose cleared her throat and willed herself to meet his eye. 'You're being melodramatic…'

'*Don't you dare accuse me of being melodramatic!*' Gabriel bellowed, leading her to fear that in a minute the rest of the office would come hurtling through the outside door to see what the commotion was all about. He stood up and placed both his hands squarely on his desk, every muscle in his body rigid with threat. He couldn't have felt more shocked by her resignation than if he had walked into his office only to find a gaping hole waiting for him instead.

'I let you go to Australia,' he thundered, 'at massive inconvenience to myself…'

Rose, unwilling as she was to wave any red flags in front of charging bulls, was not about to let Gabriel get away with implying that she had cleared off for three months and left him in the lurch. In fact, she could count on the fingers of one hand the number of times she had not been available for him. She had worked late more evenings than she cared to remember, had eaten takeaway food in front of her desk way after the rest of the workforce had departed, had cancelled friends at short notice so as not to let him down.

'I arranged a perfectly good stand-in for you in my absence,' she pointed out quietly.

'You arranged to have an emotional wreck take over! A woman who spent the duration of her appointment to me on the brink of a nervous breakdown! Not my idea of a perfectly good stand-in!'

'And the rest of them?' Rose hung on to her temper with difficulty.

'Useless. Surprised they could find jobs anywhere. Can't imagine what that agency was thinking, having them on their books.'

'Maybe you should have looked at the pattern,' Rose murmured under her breath but not so softly that Gabriel didn't hear exactly what she said.

'What are you trying to say?' he roared and Rose jumped and glanced nervously over her shoulder.

'Nothing!' she said placatingly.

Wrong move. If anything, her attempts to soothe had stoked his anger even further and he shot out of his chair and moved round the desk to where she was sitting, pressed back against the soft tan leather, hands clenched on her lap.

'Well!' He leaned over the chair until his face was thrust aggressively into her line of vision. Rose flinched.

She had known that her letter of resignation would not meet with a favourable response. She was good at her job and over the years Gabriel had become accustomed to her. They worked together in perfect harmony, often barely needing to verbally communicate in order to understand what the other meant. Unlike the secretaries he had had in the past, Rose had never been afraid of him. She had witnessed his rage at some piece of incompetence or other presented to him by one of his employees and had always managed to deflate it, usually by ignoring it altogether.

Her unflappability, she knew, meant a lot to him. And Gabriel would not appreciate the huge change to his routines which her resignation would engender. His private life might be colourful and ever changing but he liked his working life to be ruthlessly ordered and part of the order, she knew, was her predictable presence.

'I'm waiting!'

'I'm not going to say a word until you…stop leaning over me, Gabriel. You're making me feel…*threatened*…'

'What do you think I'm going to do?' Involuntarily, his eyes raked over her breasts, noticing the hint of cleavage he could see in the deep V of her T-shirt. When she didn't answer, he pushed himself away from her and raked his fingers through his black hair in frustration.

Rose instantly felt her breathing get back to somewhere near normal. 'Every one of those temps couldn't have been hopeless, Gabriel.' He glanced at her over his shoulder and their eyes met. 'You intimidate people. You probably intimidated them.'

'Me? Intimidate people?' He resumed his position, perched on his desk so that he was staring down at her. 'Maybe, occasionally,' he admitted reluctantly. 'But in the world of business, you know that a little intimidation can be a very handy tool. Is that why you're leaving? Because you just don't like working for me?' Gabriel frowned, trying to make sense of the incomprehensible. She had been happy enough with her work when she had departed for Australia. Now, here she was, suddenly keen to head off to greener pastures.

Not that they existed. As far as Gabriel was concerned, she was on to a damn good deal working for him. Salary wise, she would be hard pressed to match it at any other company in London. Probably in the country, for that matter.

He wondered what that sister of hers had said to her about her job in London. Holed up in some rural retreat in the outback, she had probably been keen to encourage Rose into a similar situation, maybe dump the fast pace of city life in favour of something a little more laid back.

'Has that sister of yours tried to persuade you that leaving London is a good idea…?' He frowned as the pieces of the puzzle began reforming in his head. 'Don't tell me that you're stupid enough to consider moving to Australia!' Shock mixed with something else ripped through Gabriel like a jolt of electricity. 'Just because your only living relative happens to be there! And what if she decides to move somewhere else? What if that husband of hers gets a transfer to somewhere even more unlikely? Do you pull up your roots and follow them?' He snorted with disbelieving laughter.

'If I'm that stupid, then why the fuss if I leave?'

'Stop fishing for compliments, Rose.' Gabriel began pacing the room and Rose watched his restless progress out of the corner of her eye until he was back behind his desk, reclining back in the leather chair so that he could look at her with accusatory disapproval. 'You know I value what you do for me. I don't need to say it. Are you planning on going to Australia?' For some reason he found that he didn't care for the thought of that at all. He tried to imagine her forging a life in the outback, stuck in the middle of nowhere. But then, she wouldn't be forging it on her own, would she? Hooded blue eyes took in the now slim figure in front of him, her skin bronzed and glowing from three months spent in the sun, her brown hair shiny with copper highlights and falling in a thick, blunt bob to her shoulders. No, some Neanderthal outback rancher would be all too happy to play caveman to her. That thought made his teeth snap together and he frowned at her.

'No,' Rose informed him wearily. 'I'm not planning on moving out to Australia and I know you value what I do here.'

'Then why?' He gave one brief scathing glance at the offensive letter lying on his desk. 'One polite paragraph is all I deserve after being an exemplary and generous boss to you over four years?'

'I didn't think you would like flowery speeches. And there

was nothing more to say, anyway. I really am leaving because I think there are still things out there left to do and I can't do them while I'm working here, even though, yes, you've been a very generous boss.'

'Things left to do?' Gabriel frowned.

'I…yes…'

'What things?'

'A business course, as a matter of fact…' Among other things, she thought, such as developing a life of my own, a life that included finding a suitable mate, settling down, having a family, doing all the things most women dreamed of from a young age.

'You want to do *a business course?*' He made it sound as though she had just revealed a secret yearning to fly to the moon.

'As a matter of fact, I do!' Rose tilted her chin up defensively, her normally serene face flushed with sudden annoyance that he found it so incredulous that she should have ambitions outside the ones he so kindly allowed her. 'I left home at eighteen,' she snapped, revealing yet more of a life she had previously been keen to keep under wraps, 'to look after my mother and when she passed on I did a secretarial course, took a series of temporary jobs just so that I could get sufficient funds together to put myself through a really good intensive course… If you recall, I came to *you* as a temp…and ended up staying here permanently…'

'You never said…' Gabriel murmured, reading the dismay on her face as she contemplated her outburst. So his cool, calm, level-headed secretary had fire burning inside. Of course he'd suspected that from the very start. 'What was your sister up to while you were looking after your mother?' he asked curiously, sidetracked by that window into her private life.

Rose looked at his devilishly handsome face and tried to

wriggle back to her secure guarded territory but he was having none of it. After a few seconds of thick, expectant silence, she shrugged and looked away. 'Grace was at university and then she met Tom and everything got...very hectic for her. So. Anyway, that's one of the things I want to do...'

'And you've checked out these business courses?'

'Well...'

'No point spending time doing a business course only to find that it qualifies you to bounce right back here...'

'Thanks for the tip, Gabriel. I'll make sure I'm very careful what sort of course I sign up to.'

He was looking at her thoughtfully, so thoughtfully that her antennae pricked up, waiting for some passing remark which she suspected she wouldn't like.

'Naturally, I'll work out my notice,' she ventured into the lengthening silence. No response. She plunged on, wondering whether this silent tactic was designed to make her feel guilty. He certainly wouldn't be beyond using every trick in the book to get her to stay, if that was his goal, especially now that he had a benchmark for comparison after three months of unsatisfactory stand-ins. 'I intend to take just a couple of months off after I leave here, enjoy the summer...maybe even go abroad somewhere...and then the course will start in September...'

'And it never occurred to you that we could discuss this...? Maybe arrive at a conclusion satisfactory to both of us...?'

'Not really. I mean...'

'Why not?' Gabriel was in there like a shot. 'Because underneath it all, you have a problem with working for me?'

'Of course not!' The last thing she needed, not that it mattered, was to leave Gabriel with the ego boosting impression that he had an effect on her.

'Then why didn't you come and discuss your dilemma with me?'

'I really only thought about it when I was in Australia,' Rose admitted. 'I had time to think out there and to realise that I needed a change if I was to advance my career…'

Gabriel, struggling with the prospect of a litany of incompetent secretaries cowering and ducking for cover every time he raised his voice, mentally cursed her absent sister once again for introducing strife into his otherwise perfectly uncomplicated working life.

'And I agree with you,' he told her suddenly.

'You do?'

'Of course I do.' He leaned back, linking his fingers behind his head, and surveyed her with an expression of sympathetic understanding that she had never seen in evidence before. 'You're young. You're clever…' He allowed the throwaway compliment to sink in. 'You want a career beyond taking orders from me. Not,' he felt compelled to add, 'that I haven't given you your fair share of responsibility. In fact, considering your original duties were filing, typing and fending calls, you've come a long way. But that's by the by…'

Rose tried to keep up with this surprising twist. Not that Gabriel wasn't unpredictable. He was. She just hadn't anticipated any such reaction to her resignation because, really, how many ways were there to react to a resignation letter? And so he was now accepting it. Why feel disappointed with an outcome she knew was inevitable?

'I can understand your drive to go further… After all, I am a perfect example of someone who has been there, someone who was driven to better himself…'

'I don't plan on dizzy heights…'

'Did I ever tell you that my parents started with nothing?

That my father's business began with dabbling in the rag trade? Just enough money to raise us without too much hardship but not so much that we didn't know from very young the importance of an education and the importance of making the most of our talents?'

'Don't worry, Gabriel, I won't be competing with you on your level in two years' time…!'

Their eyes met in perfect understanding as he appreciated the gentle, teasing irony behind her remark and Rose looked away quickly. He might not have much inside information about her private life but in many ways he knew her better than anyone else ever had and certainly cottoned on to her quirky sense of humour quicker than anyone she had ever known. Even Grace had seemed left behind sometimes.

'If you had told me sooner I would have happily arranged to fund your course.'

'I'm sorry?'

'Day release. Even two days a week. You keep the salary you're at and the only condition is that you train up someone to fill in for you when you're not here. And, when your course is complete, I guarantee you a junior position on the top floor. I was also thinking of rewarding your efforts here with a company car…'

'I'm not sure…'

'So we're back to that *invisible reason* for quitting and since it's nothing to do with what I have to offer by way of benefits, then it must have something to do with me…'

'I told you, of course not!'

'Then why don't you give it a go, Rose…?' Gabriel leaned forward and rested his elbows on the desk. 'I don't want you to go…' His navy-blue eyes swept over her in a way that felt almost like a caress and Rose shivered with guilty pleasure.

I don't want you to go—lover's words. 'I need you,' he compounded the ambiguous intimacy of his previous plea with a husky murmur. 'If the arrangement doesn't suit you, then you can leave me. No hard feelings.' Then he did something he had never done before. He said *please*.

CHAPTER TWO

THE following morning found Rose on the phone, frantically trying to do some research into business management courses. When she had vaguely mentioned her desire for a change in career to Gabriel, she had had no idea that she would have been called to account. Yes, somewhere in the recesses of her mind, she had toyed with the idea of gaining a couple more qualifications, but really her decision to leave had been based on more pragmatic grounds. She had just thought it time to disentangle herself from Gabriel's pervasive influence over her life.

Somehow she had been manoeuvred into the unenviable position of embarking on a course, which she had supposedly checked out in depth. In addition to this technical hiccup, she would now have to set about recruiting someone to fill in for her when she wasn't around.

When she had discussed her situation with Grace, resignation had seemed the most appropriate solution and thousands of miles away, with a warm Australian sun beating down and the thought of London and her job like a hazy dream, she had imagined a clean cut conclusion. Her letter of resignation, some surprise on Gabriel's part and a valiant attempt to persuade her out of her decision, but of course in her head she never wavered. Roll on two years and she could easily see herself in a fulfilling relationship with a mystery man, someone kind and thoughtful, with the sound of wedding bells clanging on the horizon.

She hadn't banked on the reality of actually walking back in to her office, seeing him again for the first time in three months. She hadn't taken into account how devastating his smile could be and she certainly hadn't envisaged her big, powerful boss with his killer looks gazing at her in that pleading manner and begging her to stay.

She thanked heaven that he was out of the office for the day, giving her ample opportunity to begin researching courses. So far only two stood out as worth pursuing as they seemed to offer what she thought she wanted and both were within fairly easy commuting distance. By the time lunchtime rolled around she had arranged to see both towards the end of the week.

Keeping her afloat whenever she contemplated the rapid desertion of her cause was the thought that she had only promised Gabriel *to give it a go,* leaving her the option of walking away after three months if she chose.

She was still at her desk at six-thirty, playing catch-up with all the work she had pushed to one side having spent the morning on the phone to colleges.

She was hardly aware of Gabriel until his shadow on her desk alerted her to his presence, then she glanced up, involuntarily sucking in her breath as their eyes met.

'I guess you missed this…' He raised his eyebrows and grinned. 'Hence the fact that you're still here slaving away while everyone else has gone…' He dumped an assortment of files on her desk. 'A few more bits to keep you busy but you can sort them out tomorrow. One or two problems with that new build hotel in the Caribbean. We need to source a more reliable supplier. Roberts in Barbados should be able to help you with that one.' He moved round to see what she was doing on her computer and Rose breathed a sigh of relief that he hadn't found her scrolling down colleges in the London area.

'This is what I missed,' he murmured with heartfelt sincerity. 'Your efficiency. Knowing that I could leave the office and not return to find things in utter chaos and some bloody incompetent woman weeping behind her desk somewhere.'

Rose clicked off her screen and gritted her teeth together. And that was just what *she* hadn't missed! His never-ending appreciation of her as his perfect secretary.

'Which is why I would like to take you out to dinner tonight.'

Her head swung round as she edged out of her chair, taking care to avoid making physical contact with him in the process.

'I beg your pardon?'

'I'm inviting you out to dinner,' Gabriel repeated, taken aback at her patent lack of enthusiasm. 'You've been out of the country for three months...' He frowned and tried hard to suppress his annoyance at her studiously blank expression. 'There are work matters to discuss and there is no way we would get the concentrated time to discuss them in the office.'

'Well...'

'If I don't bring you up to speed with things, you'll find yourself left behind and the last thing I need is to have to set aside yet more time during the working day to sort things out.'

'Of course,' Rose said politely. 'I'll just fetch my jacket.' She logged off the computer, aware of his eyes following her every movement, and was self-consciously aware of her body as she stuck on her black linen jacket, a recent purchase that was just right for the fairly warm late spring weather.

Along with her change in shape had come a change in wardrobe. Out had gone the frumpish size fourteen clothes she had once hidden behind and in their place was an array of size tens, clothes with shapes and textures and colours she had never really been able to carry off before.

'I'd rather we weren't too late, though,' she said, bending down to scoop up her handbag which was on the floor by her desk. 'I still have unpacking to do. And you needn't worry about me falling behind with my work. I intend to spend the weekend at home with some of the files making sure that I know exactly what's going on with all our accounts.'

'Right.'

'Where are we going to eat?' Rose glanced down at her working clothes. 'I'm not really dressed for anywhere too fancy.' And Gabriel didn't really do cheap and cheerful. Not because he was a crashing snob but because he never really had any need to. She should know. She had booked enough restaurants for him in the past to realise that gingham table-cloths and bare floorboards were not his style. Something a little wicked stirred inside her.

'I know a very good Italian,' she said, pausing to look at him. 'And it's close to where I live so I can get home relatively quickly once we're done...'

'Fine.' Gabriel was already regretting his invitation. It had not been meant as a working dinner, despite what he had said, and he now felt as though he had been pushed into a corner, forced to gear everything towards business when really he wanted to unwind and, if he were honest with himself, find out a bit more about the woman who had gone to Australia and returned completely changed.

'You don't mind, do you?'

Gabriel shrugged. 'One restaurant is as good as another when it comes to discussing work.'

He called his driver to collect them from the front of the

building and discovered that he was only marginally interested in what Rose had to ask about what had been happening in the office during her absence.

By the time they had reached the restaurant a solid forty minutes later, having waged war with the late evening traffic that had reduced some of the roads to gridlock, he was mightily fed up with discussing mergers and acquisitions. He was even more fed up with the interested but impersonal tone of her chatter. He couldn't remember ever having had such a pressing urge to get behind the smoothly calm surface and see what lay there.

'I hope this isn't too casual for you, Gabriel.'

Gabriel narrowed his eyes and tried to work out whether there was a certain insolence in her voice, although when he looked at her she just seemed politely concerned.

'Why should it be too casual?' he asked as they entered the restaurant. It was more of a pub than a restaurant, with after work people milling around by the bar area, while others were seated at wooden tables in small, animated groups. And, to his surprise, Rose seemed to be known at the place. Someone materialised out of thin air, smiling and kissing her on both cheeks before showing them to a table tucked away at the very back.

'Because I know you tend to like more expensive places.'

'Oh, do I?'

'Yep.' She turned to him and smiled dryly. 'Don't forget I book them for you.' She lowered her eyes and slipped into her seat. 'Beautiful women like expensive restaurants, you once said. They enjoy the goldfish bowl feeling, hence you go to places where seeing who's there is half the fun.'

'I once said *that?*'

'You did.'

'I'm surprised you didn't accuse me of being shallow.'

Rose shrugged, glanced at him and glanced away. 'Each to their own. Besides, I work for you.'

'That's never stopped you from speaking your mind.'

Rose flushed and remained silent. Yes, she had always spoken her mind, had never been scared to disagree with him and he had allowed her to be as open as she felt. Was that one of the reasons why her emotions had become involved, even though she had tried desperately hard to rein them in? He might be a hard task master, with almost zero tolerance of anything that smacked of laziness or stupidity, but he was also the fairest man she had ever met and willing to listen to anyone's opinions, provided they could be backed up. It was an immensely persuasive side of his personality and one to which she had been exposed for four long years.

'Is this your local?' Gabriel asked, changing the subject. He looked around and, after a few minutes, his gaze finally rested on her. 'I didn't imagine that this would be your kind of place.'

'Why is that?' Rose answered with asperity.

'Because…it's pretty noisy.'

'And I'm more of a library kind of person?'

'You're putting words into my mouth, Rose.'

'I'm tired.' She was grateful for the waiter's interruption, placing her order without bothering to look at the menu. 'Why don't you fill me in on what's been happening? I know a bit from your emails, but if you give me some details it'll be easier for me to catch up.'

'That Australia flight's a long one,' Gabriel said, avoiding the subject of work, which seemed unutterably boring just at the moment. 'I can understand why you're tired. And I expect you miss your sister as well, hmm…?'

'Yes. Of course I do. Although they're planning on returning to England to live some time next year. Both of them feel it's time to come back home now that baby Ben is on the scene.'

Their food arrived and Rose was amused to see surprise register on Gabriel's face as he noted the quality of the dishes. He looked up, caught her eye before she could look away, and grinned.

'Now I'm going to get a sermon on the foolishness of people who pay over the odds for a meal they can easily get somewhere else at half the price...'

'No, of course not.'

'I would come to places like this if it weren't for the fact that clients and women expect more elaborate entertaining.'

'I can understand the clients, but maybe you need to mix with a different kind of woman.'

'Why do you say that?'

'Say what?'

Rose, who had not really been paying much attention to what she had been saying, looked up to find his midnight-blue eyes fixed on her. Weren't they supposed to be talking about work? Wasn't that the whole point of them being here?

'I've never really known what you think about my... women...but I guess you must have had opinions on them over the years. After all, you've met them all...'

'Not really...' Oh, yes, she had opinions on them! Beautiful, empty-headed, utterly unthreatening. For a long time she used to wonder how a man as dynamic and astute as Gabriel could ever be interested in the stereotype of the blonde bimbo. Yes, she could understand his need to have a beautiful woman on his arm. Like attracted like, after all. But wouldn't he have been more challenged by a woman who had something to say for herself? Then gradually she had realised the simple truth, which was that he didn't *want* to be challenged. He got enough challenge with his work. What he wanted was docility. When he eventually decided to settle down, he would doubtless want that same docility from a woman who would be content to serve him, have his children and patiently stand by while he worked all the hours God made. Behind the passion and seduction of his work, he would require a soothing, calming domestic life.

'Is that why you're looking at me with such disapproval?' Gabriel asked and Rose caught herself with a little start. While she grappled with the dilemma of working out how to lead the conversation back into safe waters, Gabriel seized the moment to press her for an answer.

'Was I?'

'Oh, yes. Your little mouth was pursed tightly with disapproval!'

Rose glared at him and he grinned back at her, knowing very well that his description would have got under her skin. It wasn't like him to tease. Up until now she had rebuffed every effort he had ever made to move their relationship on to a more cordial basis and he had obligingly backed off, but something had changed and, although he couldn't put his finger on it, he knew that he was rather enjoying the change.

He smiled down into the glass of wine he was cradling in his hand. She had stuck to water but, with a driver waiting patiently for him outside, he had decided to have a couple of drinks.

'What you do in your private life is entirely up to you.' Rose heard the primness in her voice with mounting irritation. 'If you choose to go out with women whose IQs are in single figures, then that's your business!'

'Ah. I never took you for an intellectual snob,' Gabriel murmured in an infuriatingly meek voice.

'I am *not* an intellectual snob!' Rose defended hotly.

'And how,' Gabriel continued with pseudo-thoughtfulness, 'can you condemn women who like having money lavished upon them unless you've been in that position before?' He paused. 'Have you?'

'No, but…'

'I mean, how do you know that you wouldn't enjoy being taken to the finest restaurants? Having pearls and diamonds bought for you? Being flown to Paris or Venice for the weekend?'

'I don't recall booking too many flights to Paris or Venice for weekend jaunts,' Rose said tartly. Gabriel had no problem in spending vast sums of money on gifts for the women who came and went in his life but setting aside time for them was an entirely different thing. He rarely had time off and when he did he invariably went back to Italy to visit family. She should know. She didn't think he had ever booked a flight himself.

'You know what I mean,' Gabriel said irritably.

Torn between abandoning the conversation and standing up for herself, Rose took the plunge and for once set aside her determination to keep her thoughts to herself. 'I don't *have* to have expensive things bought for me to know that it wouldn't be what I wanted. My parents both instilled in us a healthy awareness that money doesn't buy happiness.'

'Oh, I know that money can't buy *happiness,*' Gabriel agreed readily. 'At least not happiness of the lasting kind, but it can buy fun…'

'Depends if you think fun is having a six-month fling, dusting yourself down and moving on,' Rose muttered.

'I take it *you* don't think it is…'

'This is a ridiculous conversation. Weren't we supposed to be talking about work? Apparently, I need to be *brought up to speed* just in case I get left behind.'

Gabriel knew damn well that his comment had been totally

unjustified, but hell, he had invited the woman out to dinner only to find that she had no desire to go so apologising wasn't on his list of priorities. Nor was discussing work. He couldn't think of anything duller than discussing acquisitions, profit and losses, breakdowns in supply and demand with one of his hotels, not when the alternative was so much more interesting.

'There's no chance that you'll get left behind, Rose,' he said placatingly. He nodded to the waiter to clear their plates and when another glass of wine was offered he looked enquiringly at her dubious expression.

'Please don't tell me that that nasty concept called *fun* also includes the occasional bit of alcohol...' That, he was pretty sure, would really get her bristling, and it did.

'Of course I have a drink now and again! I do have a *life* outside work, Gabriel.'

'Tell me about it.' He was in there like a shot, having dispatched the waiter to bring them a glass of wine each. Large. 'No boyfriends with lavish spending habits—that would be unhealthy and bad for the soul...'

Rose opened her mouth to respond and then shut it. Instead she gave him a wry look. 'The devil finds work for idle hands, Gabriel. I feel very sorry for those poor girls if you were like this with them.'

'Like what?' Gabriel asked piously.

'Barbing them.'

'None of them would have been equipped to handle it.'

'Or maybe you respected them more...' Rose insinuated quietly.

'Don't be bloody ridiculous. Is that what you really think? That I don't respect you? Or are you just fishing?' When she didn't answer, he raked his fingers through his hair and gave her a brooding, frustrated look. 'They were bloody useless, the lot of them. I meant it when I said that I needed you, Rose. I do.' His magnificent blue eyes flicked over her and he added, wickedly, 'Need you and want you…' He watched slow colour infuse her cheeks.

Rose, accustomed to his brilliance, his impatience and his temper, which was seldom directed at her, was thrown off balance by his flirtatious charm, something which she had always assumed was abundant but reserved for the women he dated. She didn't like it. It made her feel vulnerable and uneasy and she stoically hung on to her composure and managed to say, without any inflection whatsoever in her voice, 'You think you do, Gabriel, but no one is indispensable, least of all a secretary.' She sipped her wine and eyed him over the rim of her glass.

'Don't underestimate yourself.'

'I'm not. But I'm not about to think that your working life will grind to a halt if I'm not around.'

'Maybe not *grind to a halt*,' Gabriel admitted. 'But run considerably less smoothly. I've spent the past three months finding that out.' He was amused to realise that she had never voiced her opinions to him about the women in his life. He also realised that, without using so many words, she had managed to imply distaste with how he conducted his private life. Belatedly it occurred to him that she had widely overstepped the mark with her smugness and she had got away with it. How did that follow when he prided himself on being a man who knew exactly where to draw his verbal boundaries? Healthy criticism on the work front was fine. In fact, to be encouraged! His personal life was, however, his own business and not up for discussion. He chose to disregard the little voice in his head telling him that he had solicited her opinion. It was not really fair now if he castigated her for having one because he didn't like it.

She had moved on, though. Was defining the role of secretary and why it was a position relatively easy to fulfil.
Sounding like a member of the Personnel department giving
advice to a prospective interviewee.

Gabriel grunted non-commitally.

'Basically,' she concluded, 'if I'm to be successful recruiting someone, then you need to tell me exactly what you're
looking for.'

'Recruiting someone?'

'For the days when I'm at college.'

'How many days would that be?'

'I…I'll be able to tell you that by the end of the week and
I can start recruiting in a few weeks' time.'

'Naturally, you will have to continue managing sensitive
clients and anything that might be of a confidential nature.'
He signalled for the bill and contemplated the dispiriting
prospect of a never-ending train of incompetent girls scuttling
around, trying and failing to keep up with him. 'The key
quality I'm looking for is an ability to function without
behaving like terrified little rabbits every time I speak.'

'We've been through that,' Rose said patiently. She glanced
at her watch and realised that it was a lot later than she had
imagined. And they still hadn't touched upon all that work
which apparently she needed to be filled in on. 'We haven't
got down to discussing work,' she pointed out.

'And now you have to go? Or else you might turn into a
pumpkin?' He frowned and tapped in the pin number for his
card. 'I'll drop you back to your house.'

'No need. I live within walking distance.'

'Nonsense. I would never let a woman walk back to her
house at night.'

'I do it every single day, Gabriel! Do you think I take taxis to and from work? The bus stops just down from here and I walk to my house quite safely, no matter how dark it is.' She didn't really know why she was bothering to protest because Gabriel always did what he wanted to do. Right now he wanted to play the gentleman and drop her back to her house.

'You need a car,' he said abruptly.

Rose stopped dead in her tracks and looked at him with her mouth open. 'I need a *what?*'

'A car. A company car. The fact that you haven't got one has been an oversight on my part.'

'You must be desperate to hang on to me,' she said wryly, 'if you're now offering me a car...'

'It's not exactly unusual for a PA to have a company car.' He held open the car door for her to slide in. 'Where do you live?'

Rose gave his driver the directions. Today was proving to be a day of firsts for her and she was uneasily aware that a number of them didn't sit well with her. This was the first time Gabriel had managed to crash through her carefully maintained barriers. No, they hadn't shared confidences over a bottle of wine but he had seen her professional mask slip and that wasn't good. It was also the first time he had flirted with her. Or at least spoken to her in that velvety, amused voice that she had only ever heard him use occasionally on the phone to one of his women. It was also the first time they had shared a meal together in a restaurant, just the two of them with no particular work agenda driving the occasion. None of these firsts did anything to soothe her frayed nerves at being back in his company after three months.

It was odd but it almost felt as if a door between them had opened. Over the years she had managed to cope with her feelings for him by being very careful to make sure that their roles were defined. He was her boss, a man she respected, got along well with but ultimately a man who gave her orders which she was obliged to follow. Over time, as they had grown into one another, his orders had stopped resembling orders but she had never deluded herself into thinking that she was anything to him but a very useful tool.

Some of the things she had been requested to do, as far as she was concerned, went beyond the bounds of secretarial duties. Presents for some of his girlfriends, flowers at the end of an affair, bookings for restaurants. She had done them without argument, however. She had never volunteered an opinion and he had never asked her for one. Tonight, some of those barriers had been eroded and Rose felt like a snail suddenly deprived of its protective shell.

Just thinking about it made her skin tingle and she was relieved when, after just a few minutes, the car pulled up outside her house. She pushed open her door, smiling a very hurried thank you, and was only aware that he had followed her up to her front door when he reached down to take the bundle of keys out of her fingers.

'My mother always told me to see a lady to her front door. You're trembling.'

'It's a little chilly out here.' Rose watched his long fingers as he turned the key in the lock. 'I think I must have become accustomed to the milder weather in Australia.' He handed her back the keys and their fingers brushed. 'Well—' Rose planted herself in the doorway and stared at him in a no nonsense manner '—goodnight and thank you once more for the dinner. I'm sorry we didn't get around to discussing work-related issues. Perhaps I could check your diary for the next week or so and slot in a convenient time for us to go through the problem areas…?'

'I'll leave a note about which files you need to check on

your desk and you can have a look at them some time during the day, when you get a free moment.' He placed one foot in the doorway but Rose didn't notice. She was too busy frowning and trying to work out why he had invited her out if the work issue could have been solved by way of a note on her desk.

'You could have told me that in the first place, Gabriel!'

'True,' he was quick to admit. 'But I really wanted to discuss the matter of your temporary replacement with you.'

'I won't be starting my course until September, in all probability! There's no urgency for the interviewing process to begin as yet! We're only in May.'

'The end of May,' Gabriel said darkly. 'Before you blink, we're in July and you know how normal life stops in summer with people clearing off on holiday. After the fine examples of the possibilities on offer, I would say that the interviewing process needs to begin sooner rather than later.'

Rose released a frustrated sigh.

'Have you a problem with that?'

'No. Not at all. You pay my salary. How can I have a problem with that?' She smiled to make a joke of it, but there was no answering humour in his eyes.

'In other words, what I pay you buys your compliance even if you don't agree with what I'm asking you to do.'

His remark was so close to what she had only been thinking herself minutes earlier that she blushed and looked down, to see where his foot was firmly planted.

'I'm beginning to think that all this talk about wanting to move forward your career and being held back professionally by working for me is just so much nonsense…' He wedged his foot a little more firmly through the doorway and leaned against the door frame, arms folded, his expression one of calculating suspicion. 'I smell mutiny in the ranks and experience has taught me that mutiny usually arises from personal grounds...'

'You're being over-imaginative, Gabriel...' She licked her lips nervously and wondered where he was going with this one. 'If I had...any personal problems with working for you, I would have told you...'

'Would you?' He pushed himself past her, taking her by surprise. 'Money can buy loyalty, but loyalty that's only skin-deep, and that's no good to me.' He turned to her and Rose was forced to marvel at the speed with which he had managed to get inside her house and was dwarfing its small confines.

'Can we discuss this in the morning?'

'Why? You know, it's actually only a little before nine. You'll recover from jet lag quicker if you try and maintain your normal waking times. And anyway, if there's an under-lying problem I want to hear about it.'

'I told you...' She hoped that she was the only one who could detect the desperation in her voice.

'I would never have stopped you from saying what you thought...' Gabriel said slowly, his eyes raking over her em-barrassed face. 'And I'm insulted that you would think me such an autocrat that you might be scared to voice your opinions in case I sacked you...or cut your salary...'

'Of course I didn't think that!'

Gabriel could spot a sincere answer when he heard one. Anyway, he was pretty sure she knew him better than to think that he might really try to control her with her pay cheque, but she had given him pause for thought. Starting with her letter of resignation and ending with remarks which, in a way he couldn't put his finger on, carried the ghost of criticism in them. Something in the tone of her voice and the lowering of her eyes had pricked his curiosity. Curiosity was an untapped emotion for Gabriel. The frenetic pace of his work life got his adrenalin flowing but he had been in the game long enough for uncertainty and nerves to have disappeared. He ran his empire with the confident hand of a master horseman controlling the reins of his animal. And there was no woman who incited his curiosity. Interest, yes, lust, definitely, but curiosity, not at all.

So he was like a dog with a bone now, especially since he had long ago formed very preconceived notions of his efficient secretary, notions which were in the process of being dismantled.

'Why don't you make us both a cup of coffee…?'

'No!'

'Because underneath all the *yes, sirs* and *no, sirs* and *three bags full, sirs* you can't really stand to be cooped up with me for any length of time?'

That was so far from the truth that Rose burst out laughing and after a while Gabriel grudgingly allowed his bunched muscles to relax.

'Okay. Maybe a quick cup of coffee. I wouldn't want to keep your driver waiting.' She headed towards the kitchen, mentally adding another *first* to the stack already piling up. A first for Gabriel coming inside her house. She knew that he had gone outside to tell his driver that there would be a wait. She intended to make it a short one. By the time he came back, the coffee was made, black, no sugar, as he liked it.

Rose was sitting at her kitchen table and had placed his mug conveniently at the opposite end.

'So, talk to me,' Gabriel commanded, sitting down.

'When do you want me to start interviewing for someone? Would next Monday do? Or sooner?'

'Explain your remark about obeying me because of the money.'

'I'm sorry I said that. I didn't mean it.'

'How long have you thought that way? Since you started working for me? In the last few months? Only since you got back from seeing your sister? When?'

Rose nearly groaned aloud. 'It doesn't matter, Gabriel.'

'It does to me. Now tell me what it is that you have disagreed with? You can talk to me. You'll find that I can be very sympathetic. I don't want to lose you and if you've been harbouring any grudges about the way I run things, then now is the time to get it off your chest.'

CHAPTER THREE

THE restaurant in the glass office building, like everything else, was fairly spectacular. It was one of the invisible but very handy perks that came with working for Gabriel. It was open all day, served a staggering choice of first class food and was so heavily subsidised that loose change could buy a hefty enough breakfast to last the day.

Every so often Gabriel, when he wasn't entertaining clients or being entertained by them, would emerge from his glorified sanctum and stroll down for lunch. He did it to *touch base* with his employees. Rose always smiled at that because *touching base* with his employees was a pretty ridiculous notion when it came to Gabriel Gessi. He chatted to them, invited their ideas, and they chatted back. But scratch the surface and it was easy to see the awe that controlled their replies. He wasn't just rich and powerful but he looked the part and that in itself was enough to make most of his employees break out in a light nervous perspiration.

Right now, at two-thirty in the afternoon, the lunch time stampede had come and gone. Over by the windows were two small groups of people—three girls from the kitchens, who were having cups of coffee and doughnuts, and a couple of men who were talking animatedly over sheets with graphs and figures.

Aside from that, it was empty. Perfect conditions for Rose to sip from her mug of coffee and morosely mull over events of the night before.

He had asked her for her opinions and to start with she had had no trouble resisting the invitation. Four years of habit had come to her rescue, saving her from succumbing to the novelty of their situation and behaving in a way that would have been out of character. She had looked at him quizzically, lowered her eyes and paid a lot of attention to her cup of coffee.

He, on the other hand, had stared at her over the rim of his cup, in no particular hurry to go. Then, changing the subject, he had quizzed her about what sort of course she was interested in doing, what qualification would she achieve at the end of it, would she want a job supervising other people or working primarily on her own? Harmless questions that were just what an interested boss would ask, nothing to set her antennae quivering.

When he had asked her about her parents, what her father had done for a living, she had not flinched because the questions had been wrapped up in an intelligent observation about the influences of parents on their children.

'Based on my own parents,' he said, standing up and taking his cup to the sink, 'I should have married years ago. In fact, I'm long overdue for the two point two kids and family dog.' He grinned at her, a self-deprecatory grin that invited her to enter into light-hearted criticism of his rakish lifestyle.

'I can't picture you with two point two kids.' Rose cupped her chin in her hands and stared up at him, noting the way his big, muscular frame dominated her small kitchen. Not in her wildest flights of imagination had she once thought that her letter of resignation, her bid for a life without him, would see her sitting in her kitchen joining him in a cup of coffee as if it was the most natural thing in the world. Talk about plans being derailed! 'I can just about get my head around the dog.'

'What kind of dog?'

'A very big one.'

'Because I'm six foot two?'

Well, of course, that comment invited her to look at him and for a few seconds her heart seemed to stop beating. Six foot two of pure blue-eyed, black-haired alpha male.

'You'd better go,' she said abruptly, standing up.

'I will, in about fifteen minutes. I told Harry to go and fill the car up instead of just waiting and he won't be back yet.'

'Why did you do that?' Rose said in dismay. Now that she was on her feet, she couldn't decide whether to go across to the sink and risk an awkward situation with them both there, squashed side by side into an impossibly small space, or else ignominiously sit back down. In the end she clicked her tongue and turned on her heel, out to the sitting room cum room where everything was done, from television watching to out of hours work to reading the newspaper on a Sunday morning before she walked down to the bakery to buy her weekly treat of croissants.

'Because,' his voice came from behind her, 'it beat the hell out of sitting in the car waiting for me in the dark.'

'He could have turned the light on and read!'

'Provided he remembered to come equipped with a book.'

Rose shot him a long-suffering look, which was water off a duck's back, and sat down. 'Harry always travels with a book.'

'How do you know?'

'Because I once asked him how he tolerated having to drive you places and then wait, sometimes for hours, until you finished whatever meeting you might have been in.'

'You've been having long conversations with my chauffeur?' His tone of voice implied that she had been hiding some dirty secret from him, something which he had only just unmasked, much to his horror.

'Occasionally we walk to the bus stop together if we happen to be leaving at the same time. And there's no need to look so staggered, Gabriel. People do have lives outside your corporation.'

'I know that!'

'Well, stop acting as though whatever happens outside your little world doesn't exist.'

'I don't live in a *little world*,' Gabriel grated.

'Of course you do.' She tidied up the criticism by tossing in a generality. 'You're bound to, really. Anyone in your position would. Running a corporation as huge as yours, having to dictate to other people most of the time, snapping your fingers and knowing that you'll be obeyed. It's not the real world.'

Gabriel's eyes narrowed on her. 'I'm a petty dictator?'

'No, of course not! That's not what I said at all!'

'I give orders, I snap my fingers and expect obedience. I suppose the next step is to issue the royal command that all my subjects kneel when I walk by!'

'I'm sorry if I offended you.'

'You haven't *offended* me,' Gabriel said coolly. 'You work for me and as my employee you are entitled to an opinion and I appreciate your opinion. I only wish you had had the guts to tell me a little sooner instead of scuttling around like a mouse, smiling and obeying and harbouring unpleasant resentments.'

Rose's mouth fell open and she stared at him in horror. 'I wasn't *harbouring resentments*,' she denied, her face turning a deeper shade of red.

'No?' Gabriel felt as though he had been struck a blow

beneath the belt and he didn't like the feeling. Underneath the guise of the man who worked hard and played hard, was a man of exceptional self-control. Right now he could feel his iron control shifting and it was a very unpleasant sensation. Especially considering that the woman was no more than his secretary. A valued member of his team, yes, but still a member of his team and nothing of any worth personally to him.

'No…if I had any problems working for you…well, I would have told you…I wouldn't have *scuttled around like a mouse*…' That description hurt because she could see how he would have arrived at it. She came in, she did her job, she went home. Her own confusing emotional vulnerability as far as he was concerned had made her a more silent person than she was by nature, but how was he to know that? What he knew was a quiet, efficient woman who did her job but never said anything that might have expressed any feelings that were un-related to work. A highly competent scuttling mouse. And, three months ago, a plump little mouse.

Not for the first time, Rose was besieged by images of all the women he had dated. In her head, they marched past in a long, beautiful procession. She had met them all, or at least most of them because he would often arrange for them to meet him at the office when he had finished work, only he rarely finished when he promised and so they would sit in her office, long legs crossed, their perfect faces blank with boredom as they stared around them or tried to make small talk. Blonde, brunette, red-haired—Gabriel showed no favouritism. His only criteria was that they were gorgeous and intellectually undemanding.

Sometimes Rose would spot an item of jewellery she had bought on his behalf. A diamond bracelet, a necklace, maybe a Hermes scarf, which always went down a treat because it was somehow a little more personal than an item of jewellery, or so they imagined, unaware that Gabriel would have had nothing to do with the choosing.

She looked at him now and saw herself through his eyes. The plump mouse scuttling quietly around, doing his bidding. Little wonder she had become his perfect secretary! And even less surprising that he had been staggered when she had returned from Australia clutching her letter of resignation and sporting a whole new image. He had turned on the charm and pulled out all the financial stops, but her decision to stay had nothing to do with either of those things.

She was a different woman now. She looked different and inside she had changed. She wasn't going to scuttle any more because she had nothing to lose. She had made her mind up that her life was going down a different path and, if she happened to still be working for him, she was merely biding her time.

She liked the sound of that. *Biding her time.* It gave her a heady rush of courage.

'I have no problem working for you, Gabriel, because I'm not afraid of you. I've worked alongside you long enough to know…'

'How to handle me…?'

'How to gauge your various moods…'

'Which is good.'

Rose took in the smug expression and gritted her teeth together. 'Yes, yes, it is. Which isn't to say that I'm not going to set down a few requirements now that you have persuaded me to carry on working for you, provided it doesn't conflict with my course…I don't want you to forget that I'm going to give it three months and during that time I'll make sure I train someone up who could take over completely from me if I do decide to leave…'

Every inclination in him wanted to inform her that he was not in the market for blackmail, emotional or otherwise, but then he remembered the succession of hopeless temps and bit back the words. He didn't want Rose to leave but, if she did, he wanted to make damn sure that she sorted out someone responsible who could take over from her.

'What are your requirements? I thought I had made the financial deal enticing enough.'

'It's not to do with money, actually…' Rose drew in her breath and looked at him steadily. 'Firstly, I want to have a certain amount of notice if I'm required to work unusually late hours…'

'*A certain amount of notice?*' Gabriel exploded with disbelief. 'How much *notice* did you have in mind? A week? Two weeks? A month?' He shot out of his chair and prowled around the room, scowling. The hopeful anticipation with which he had awakened that morning had turned into grim faced frustration and was getting worse by the minute. And all because his dependable secretary had disappeared for three months and returned a hell cat. Lord only knew what thoughts that sister of hers had put in her head.

'A day or two would be sufficient,' Rose told him calmly. Her cool cream sitting room, with its small fireplace and its neatly spaced oak bookshelves on either side, seemed poky and cluttered with him in the room. Even when they were having a perfectly normal conversation, he still couldn't obey the laws of common courtesy and sit down politely, hear her out without interrupting, just behave like a normal human being!

'And would that be in writing?' Gabriel asked sarcastically.

'I'm not being unreasonable…'

'No? You mean it's common practice for someone in a responsible job, earning, might I point out, vastly more than the national average, to work to rule unless given notice?'

Rose had seen Gabriel in action before. He was physically intimidating and was not above bullying his opponents into submission.

'I wasn't implying that I would *work to rule,* Gabriel, just saying that, whilst I don't object to working late now and again, you've frequently asked me to stay on at the office, sometimes until midnight, working on documents that have a deadline.'

'*Frequently* is a bit of an overstatement,' Gabriel muttered.

'Whatever. I'm going to be occupied studying and I think it only fair that you respect that.'

'What would you classify these *unusually late hours* you refer to?'

'Anything beyond six-thirty would not be acceptable.' Rose waited for the fallout but nothing came. Instead, he looked at her assessingly and, after a few seconds pause, he shrugged.

'Fine.'

'You don't mind?'

'Well, naturally, it'll be inconvenient, but you're right. You're going to be studying. The last thing I would want to do is distract you from that…' He lowered his eyes. 'You will have to make sure that whoever replaces you is not going to be a clock-watcher.'

'You might find it difficult to locate a temp who doesn't mind staying on until whatever time you decide at the snap of a finger.' *Whoever replaces you?* There was a permanent ring to that statement and it sent a chill down her spine even though it was, of course, precisely what she had wanted in the first place.

'Not if I dangle enough money in front of her…and of

course the promise of knowing that the job might very well be hers permanently, with all the perks that go along with it.'

'You mean you're writing me off already?' Rose said lightly. 'I thought I was indispensable.'

'So did I.'

But somewhere along the line he had changed his mind. Probably when she made it clear that agreeing to stay in the job brought one or two conditions that he found unpalatable. He wanted someone who blindly obeyed, never mind the baloney about encouraging free speech with his employees. He wanted to be able to tell her, somewhere around five-thirty in the evening, that two lawyers would be coming in at six and she would have to stay on until all the nuts and bolts of some deal or other had been ironed out. He didn't want to hear anything about outside commitments and he certainly wouldn't want to give her any notice for inconvenience.

As long as she was quietly and competently invisible, all would be right in his world. Money would flow for her, company cars would be forthcoming. He neither wanted nor needed the hassle of a secretary who insisted on having a mind of her own. And Rose had passed four years obliging him on that count, keeping her thoughts firmly to herself.

'There's more,' she said, going with the motto that *in for a penny in for a pound.*

'Since when did you decide that being prickly was a helpful asset in your career?' The mildness of his tone was marred by a faintly disgruntled edge.

'I thought you welcomed your employees' opinions?' Rose said innocently.

'Of course I welcome hearing what my employees think,' Gabriel said irritably. 'And please do me a favour and don't launch into any long, boring speeches about my little world being so removed from reality that I wouldn't recognise free speech if it hit me in the face.' He looked at her, at her wry expression, and grunted. 'Well, you might as well get on with it. What more complaints have you been nurturing?'

Trust Gabriel to turn the tables, Rose thought, and translate her very valid points as below the belt stabs.

'These women of yours…'

'What women…?' It took Gabriel a few seconds to realise what she was talking about, then he narrowed his eyes cautiously. 'Don't go there, Rose.'

Rose could understand why she was in danger of becoming the Secretary from Hell. She felt a few fleeting seconds of sympathy for him. On top of her sudden demands for a change in her working hours, she was now about to inform him that taking care of his women was not part of her job specification and she would no longer be doing it. If he wanted to order flowers at the demise of a relationship, then he could phone the florist and order them himself. If he urgently needed an expensive token to compensate for cancelled dates, then he could set forth and purchase it himself.

'I need to have my say, Gabriel…'

'Which doesn't include preaching to me about the way I conduct my life outside work. That, I warn you, is way beyond your brief.' The flat, hard expression made Rose suddenly bristle. It was fine for him to ask her questions about *her* private life, to try and eke out information and then voice his opinions on the little he had managed to unearth, but he wasn't about to allow her the same freedom! Three months ago it wouldn't have occurred to her to speak her mind. In fact, the decent part of her knew that she should set him straight and tell him that she wouldn't dream of saying anything about how he conducted his private life, that the changes she had in mind were of a more practical nature, but she wasn't feeling particularly decent at the moment.

'What do you think I'm going to say, Gabriel?' She met his dark, brooding gaze evenly. 'Since you seem to be a mind-reader on top of everything else.'

'It doesn't take a genius to work out what's on your mind,' Gabriel rasped. He was beginning to regret his instinct to hang on to his wonderfully reliable secretary come hell or high water. His wonderfully reliable secretary appeared to have gone to Australia and stayed there. In her place was this forthright bordering on aggressive creature with an axe to grind and himself firmly in her sights as the grinding block.

'Oh, yes?' Rose's voice dropped by a couple of notches.

'You've made it plain that you disapprove of my behaviour towards the opposite sex. You've already said so. Of course, it hasn't crossed your mind that the women I date might actually enjoy going out with me, even if we do eventually break up.'

Rose raised her eyebrows, as if questioning his sanity in even thinking such a thing, and Gabriel glowered at her.

'I show them a good time,' he heard himself say. He wondered how it was that suddenly he was reduced to defending himself to someone whose business it most definitely was not. Or where, for that matter, that feisty look on her face had come from. 'I wine and dine them…amongst other things…' He took some satisfaction that her cool, superior expression was undermined by a slow flush. 'And believe me, Rose, when it comes to *those other things* I give a great deal of pleasure…'

'Lucky old them,' she said, recovering quickly. 'Wined, dined and bedded before being relegated to the history books.'

Gabriel was shocked. So was Rose. Where had *that* come from? She reddened and looked away but she still refused to retreat and apologise. Her sister had given her long speeches about the foolishness of falling for a man who wouldn't notice her if she stood naked on a table and danced till dawn. To him, Grace had warned darkly, Rose was a one-dimensional cut-out and always would be. Her only chance of rescuing her sense of self-worth would be to take the pay cut and leave the job.

Well, she hadn't left the job yet but she was still going to be a *woman of substance who was not afraid to speak her mind.*

'I *beg your pardon?*' Gabriel said in a shell-shocked voice, which would have been funny if she could feel anything under the rising tide of mortification.

'You heard me, Gabriel.'

'Where did you get language like *that* from?'

'Language like *what?* I don't believe I said anything obscene? Did I?'

'No, but…'

'That's fine, then!' Her sister's diagnosis of her had been brutally to the point. Rose could out-perform anyone when it came to hard work and skill. Whatever she wanted to do, Grace had said, she would achieve because she was clever and ambitious. *Unlike yours truly,* she had added ruefully. But underneath the brisk, capable exterior lurked a heart longing for romance. Hence her feelings for her boss, which she had allowed to run unchecked for four years. Like a complete idiot. Grace, so impractical when it came to anything involving office work, computers, money and all things electronic, was utterly practical in affairs of the heart. She had never wasted time mooning over unattainable boys at school and Rose was inclined to follow her advice. After all, comparing situations, who was in the better one?

'But actually I don't care what you do with the women who

come in and out of your life. What I care about is how it impacts on mine.'

'And how does it do that?' Gabriel asked with sudden interest.

'Here's how. You meet a woman. You shower her with presents. I buy the presents, usually in my lunch hour or at the weekend. Always in my leisure time, at any rate. Then there are the restaurants that need to be booked. The flowers that have to be sent with the right messages to the right people. Sometimes I have to fend off sobbing women who haven't quite seen your point of view that it was a privilege to have gone out with you and now it's time for them to find the nearest exit door. Sometimes they seem to have been under the deluded impression that you actually *cared about them*.' Her voice implied *poor fools*.

The surprises were piling on by the minute. Gabriel had never sensed any resentment in her when it came to doing what was, as far as he had always been concerned, part and parcel of a good PA's job, namely taking care of the incidentals that he had no time to do himself. Or inclination, if he was to be perfectly truthful. So what was wrong with ordering a few flowers down the phone now and again? Or taking a trip to the jewellers to buy a bracelet? Didn't all women like buying jewellery?

'Are you *jealous?*' Gabriel's voice was silky-smooth and speculative and, in response, Rose could feel her heartbeat quicken, because, and this was a truth she only admitted to herself late at night, when she was alone with her thoughts, she *was*. Whenever she had been in those exclusive shops buying exclusive things, holding up a glittering ruby ring for inspection or twirling a cashmere scarf between her fingers, she had thought, *imagined,* that it was for her.

'Of course I'm not *jealous,*' she said coldly. 'Do you really think…' She caught herself in the nick of time.

'Really think…what?'

'Nothing.'

'No. Tell me. After all, today seems to be a day of revelations.'

Rose looked at him and wondered how he would react if she told him the truth on this day *of revelations*. If he was stunned by the revelations he had had thrown at him today, then he would go into a state of cataclysmic shock if she *really* decided to reveal all!

'All right. As you asked, do you really think that I would ever, *could ever,* be jealous of all those women you choose to date?' Rose laughed humourlessly. 'For a start, they're not the sharpest knives in the block…'

'Who ever said I wanted sharp?' Actually, Gabriel thought, whoever said I wanted to be discussing this? But it was such an unusual ride that he was driven to go along with it. The woman whose thoughts he had never seen was handing them to him now and he was strangely fascinated. In fact, he couldn't take his eyes away from her face, although he reluctantly admitted to himself that that might have had something to do with her physical transformation. 'An intelligent woman is an overrated species,' he said, flexing his arms and then strolling to inspect the books ranging the central fireplace on either side. Though not before glancing at her face to see how she had reacted to his incendiary remark. With gratifying outrage. He decided to continue, curious to see where the road would lead. 'I mean, an intelligent woman will usually end up getting on a man's nerves.' He idly slipped a book out of its nesting place, surprised to discover that it was a first edition and wouldn't have come cheap. An intelligent woman with taste. He shoved the book back in its spot and turned to look at her. 'The endless discussions…the earnestness…the sheer tedium of someone *with a point of view*…' He mimicked a yawn and was amused to see her eyes glitter dangerously. 'Have you noticed how an intelligent woman will always have a point of view and will always bang on about it, even when everyone else has nodded off with boredom?'

'Have you noticed—' Rose was drawn into the argument even though common sense told her that it was ridiculous '—how a bimbo will spout such rubbish that you can end up losing the will to live…?'

Gabriel shot her one of those slow, devastating smiles that made her curl her fists on her lap. Then he laughed out loud. When he had sobered up his blue eyes swept over her and he murmured, with wicked amusement, 'I won't deny they can sometimes spout rubbish but I assure you that when I'm in bed with one of them I never end up losing the will to live…'

Rose drew in a sharp intake of breath. He had pushed himself away from his inspection of her books and for a few heart-stopping seconds she could have sworn that he was moving in her direction, but then he sat down, his eyes lazy and satisfied as he contemplated past conquests. Stupid, stupid jealousy made her feel temporarily faint.

'And then…' she carried on, her voice glacial-cold even though something was raging inside her, 'I suppose I feel sorry for them. You might think that you treat them well, and you do, but what a woman wants goes beyond the things that money can buy.'

'Oh, really?'

'Oh, really. The bracelets and earrings are nice enough but a walk in the park is even better, as is a home-cooked meal and then chatting in front of an open fire or a trip to the seaside on a sunny day…'

'Possibly for *you*…'

'I've had enough conversations with the women you've

discarded to know that they're always more heartbroken than you think they are!' Rose said defensively, aware that she had given away too much in her careless musings. 'Have you any idea how difficult it is to placate someone who's in tears and wondering what they did wrong?'

The conversation, which had been pleasantly challenging, appeared to have taken an ugly turn and Gabriel frowned at her discouragingly. 'I don't know where we're going with this one...'

'You pressed me for an opinion...'

'Which is different from blanket criticism.' He shook his head and tried to get a handle on his self control.

'Only because you don't happen to agree with it,' Rose felt constrained to point out.

'How is it that I never spotted you for the stubborn, opinionated, bloody *maddening* woman you obviously are?' Gabriel grated.

Then you shouldn't mind getting rid of me when I've trained up a replacement, Rose thought, but she kept that to herself. For reasons best known to her, *she* wanted to be the one to leave. That way, she would prove to herself that she was in control, proactive as far as her emotional state was concerned.

She looked down to where her fingers were fiddling uselessly with her jumper and stilled them. But she didn't look at him and she remained mutinously silent, not trusting herself to be discreet when she next spoke. *Opinionated, stubborn* and *maddening* were not easy insults to gloss over with a polite smile and a change of subject.

More annoying than her sudden outburst of frank and open honesty was the prolonged silence that greeted his remark. Gabriel, however much he brought his passion to his work, was formidably controlled in his dealings with women. They never, but never, got under his skin. Rose's calm face lent his annoyance an edge of grinding frustration.

'I have no idea why any of the women I have ever gone out with would have wondered what they did wrong,' he heard himself saying just as he recognised the weakness in saying it. 'It's not as though they don't know from the very start that commitment isn't on the agenda. No one can criticise me for not being fair. The walks in the park, the home-cooked meal and the log-burning fire... Well, I don't do little domestic scenes like that because that would just give them the wrong impression. Actually, I don't think I would *ever* do little domestic scenes like that anyway.'

'Why not?' Rose reluctantly dragged her gaze away from her hands and met his eyes curiously.

'Not me,' Gabriel said abruptly. 'So, getting back to your complaints. No long hours without notice and no additional tasks beyond the call of duty.'

Rose nodded. 'Well, no additional tasks that don't...well, don't have anything to do with work. I'm sorry,' she felt obliged to add because she knew that laying down rules and regulations after four years was a bit of a nerve.

'Anything else?'

'No. That's all. And Gabriel, it's only because I shall need to prioritise my time if I'm to do a course...'

'Let's hope it's worth it.' He stood up and shoved his hands into his pockets and watched as she got to her feet, straightening her clothes. At least *that* reassuringly prim habit hadn't changed!

'It will be,' Rose assured him, walking out towards the front door. 'It'll be hard work but, at the end of it, I'll be able to really start building up a satisfying career for myself. Not,' she hastened to add, 'that I haven't been wonderfully happy working for you.'

'*With* me. And you could have fooled me after everything you've laid at my door this evening.'

They both paused by the front door at the same time. Their eyes tangled, brown eyes clashing with deep blue ones, and Rose had to steady herself by placing her hand flat on the closed door.

'So you intend to have it all, do you?' Gabriel drawled. 'The fast job, the fast car, the kids and the house husband who will stay at home and take care of everything…' He leaned against the door and looked down at her. She was sharp enough to have it all, that much was sure, but until now he would never have thought it interested her. With wry honesty, he acknowledged that he had always thought that *he* was enough for her.

'I don't know about that.' Now that he was on the point of imminent departure, she felt as if she could finally relax. 'I'm too old-fashioned to be happy with the house husband scenario.'

'You see the man as the protector, do you?'

'No, of course not! Well, not in such simplistic terms anyway.' She was mesmerised by the way the half-light in the hallway threw his face into intriguing angles.

'Why? What's wrong with simplistic terms? I agree with you. I'm the kind of man who would want to protect my woman. You'd better be careful, though. Your basic caveman isn't drawn to a woman who's just as capable as he is of hunting prey. Don't pursue too much independence—you might just find it backfires on you.'

'I would never be attracted to a man who was threatened by my independence,' Rose said a little too breathlessly for her liking, but then he *was* very close to her and not just close, but close and giving her his undivided masculine attention. Just in case he saw the jittery spark in her eyes and misinterpreted it, or rather interpreted it too accurately, she thought to throw in, 'And, for your information, I might not be feminist enough to want a house husband, but I certainly wouldn't want a *caveman*.'

'*Touché,*' Gabriel said dryly. He straightened up and so did she. He had the suddenly consuming urge to touch her, maybe stroke the side of her face. Instead he opened the door. 'But I'm not the caveman you seem to think I am when it comes to women...'

'No? You could have fooled me.'

'You really shouldn't say things like that,' he chided, leaning towards her so that her head was suddenly swimming and she felt as though her legs might buckle under her at any minute. 'I might just be tempted to prove you wrong.'

CHAPTER FOUR

SITTING at the very far corner of the staff restaurant, Gabriel had a bird's eye view of Rose, who was playing with the salad she had taken as though suspecting that something unpleasant might crawl out from under the lettuce leaves at any given moment. He had a feeling that she wasn't even really aware of the clattering of voices on her table. Frankly, she looked as though she was a million miles away, thinking about God only knew what. Maybe the fact that June was proving to be a record breaker as far as soaring summer temperatures went. For the past two weeks the sky had been cloudless, the heat reaching unbeaten highs of early eighties. London was sweltering. People were complaining, as they did whenever the weather did anything unexpected. The parks were a sea of white bodies slowly going red in the relentless sun.

Of course, here in the restaurant, it could have been a fine autumn day outside. The marvels of central air-conditioning, which was probably why the place was packed. Who wanted to leave the comfort of the cool indoors to venture out into the baking sun? The first few days of novelty value had worn off for most of his employees and the fierce heat was not proving to be worth the bother of a tube journey to the nearest patch of green.

Which in turn was why Rose had not noticed his presence, tucked away with a couple of his corporate finance people and one of the company lawyers. They were discussing the minutiae of his most recent acquisition and Gabriel had switched off from the conversation a while back. In truth, he shouldn't really be eating in the staff restaurant at all. A business lunch at the Savoy Grill had beckoned. Nothing that he couldn't delegate to his CEO, allowing himself the bird's eye view he was now shamelessly enjoying of his secretary.

He couldn't quite put his finger on what had changed between them, but something had. Their working relationship when she had departed for Australia had been exemplary. The ideal working relationship, in fact. And then she had returned and he wasn't sure if the physical change in her had kick-started something in him or whether it had been that evening spent with her, first at the restaurant and then afterwards at her house, during which he had caught tantalising glimpses of the red-blooded woman beneath the competent one-dimensional exterior.

Gabriel just didn't know. He just knew that for the past few weeks he had found his eyes straying towards her, noticing the details of her face, like the light sprinkling of freckles on her nose, the way her straight hair seemed to be streaked with a hundred different shades of brown and copper, the contrast of her clear brown eyes and much darker eyelashes.

And her body. He had caught himself thinking about her body at the most inappropriate times. In the middle of meetings. Sitting in front of his laptop in his office at home. On the telephone to a client, when he could look at her through the glass partition separating their offices, look at the way her full breasts were outlined against the flimsy dresses and thin silky cardigans the sheer summer heat compelled her to wear to work. He was beginning to have steamy thoughts about that body of hers which, until a few months ago, had been so properly concealed beneath sensible layers of dark-coloured clothes. Actually, up until a few months ago, he really hadn't been that aware that she had a body at all, at least not in the sexual sense of the word. Now he seemed to spend a good amount of his waking time on the verge of an embarrassing arousal.

To start with he had been amused at his intense reaction to her. And baffled. After all, it wasn't as though he hadn't spent the past four years in her company!

Very soon, though, irritation with himself had set in, at which point his logical brain reached its logical conclusion. He was suffering from sex deprivation. He had been without a woman for a while, at least three months. The last woman he had dated, a model called Caitlin, had been a willing and able playmate but had evidently wanted more than a man who could be relied upon for expensive gifts, expensive meals out, creative sex and not much else. His frequent cancellations had eventually brought about the inevitable showdown and he had been quietly relieved when she had finished with him.

Having diagnosed the problem, Gabriel had set about sorting out a solution with the speed and efficiency with which he addressed all problems. He had simply rifled through his little black book and extracted a name. The woman in question he had met several months previously and had since bumped into her at various social occasions. At each, she had reminded him that she would love a call and, with his unlikely attraction to his secretary causing him pause for uncomfortable thought, Gabriel had cheerfully set the groundwork for an enjoyable and distracting seduction.

Unfortunately, it had failed to work. Their first meeting had taken place at an intimate but lively club, a favourite haunt of

Gabriel's, who liked the live jazz band and the relaxed atmosphere. The flatness of the evening he could only blame on the music, which must have killed the conversation. Meeting two had been at a restaurant, no music and hence no excuse for the fact that he had struggled through the fine food and wine, glancing down at his watch often enough to make him realise that Arianna was perhaps not quite his cup of tea.

Which, he thought now, still left him with the unexpected problem of a secretary he was beginning to fancy. A secretary, he had to admit to himself, who had maintained an enviable detachment ever since that one evening during which she had opened up. She had reverted to being the cool ice queen, but with a sexy little body and a way of flicking a glance at him from under her lashes that made him want to slam shut that damned interconnecting door, grab her and have his wicked way with her on his grand mahogany desk.

Sam Stewart, his company lawyer, interrupted the pleasant daydream that involved some very satisfactory ripping of blouses and yanking down of lacy white bras with a question about the pension trust fund of a company with which they were negotiating and Gabriel surfaced to realise that he had missed most of a very important conversation. He dragged his attention back to the matter in hand, deliberately turning away from Rose, who was now standing up anyway, looking at her watch, straightening her skirt. Getting ready to head back to the office where she would keep her head dutifully down until five-thirty, at which point she would clear her desk and politely bid him good evening.

Later, much later, after an evening spent poring over reports with only some chilled wine and Mozart for company, Gabriel realised that he would have to do something about his worrying situation. Losing sleep over a woman was bad enough, but suffering lapses in his concentration during the day was beyond the pale.

The only solution to satisfying his curiosity, he reasoned to himself, would be to put it to bed. Literally. And the thought of that alone was enough to make his body harden in immediate response.

He made the call at nine-fifteen the following morning. And Rose took it, as he knew she would.

'Shouldn't you be here, Gabriel? I've double-checked the diaries and you're definitely not due for your first meeting until eleven. With the people from Shipley Crew...' Rose had checked the diaries more than just twice. She had checked it and re-checked it roughly a hundred times since she had entered her office, only to find Gabriel conspicuous by his absence.

'Cancel all my meetings for today, Rose. Frank can handle Shipley on his own or he can take Jenkins with him just in case they need any expert advice.'

'Where *are* you?' It was so unlike Gabriel to be unpredictable during working hours that Rose actually felt a physical tingle of apprehension race down her spine.

'At my place.'

'Doing what?' She took a few deep breaths and repeated the question in a less crazed voice.

'Being under the weather.'

'You're *under the weather?* As in *ill?* You're *never ill*, Gabriel!'

'Try telling that to the strep bacteria in my throat.' Which he cleared convincingly.

Rose was torn between thinking that, with typical male lack of stamina, Gabriel had caved in to the simple cold bug with which he was unfamiliar, or else he was really ill. Ill as in *should go to hospital ill*.

'You seemed fine yesterday,' Rose informed him briskly. 'Are you sure you…' she opted for the least worrying option '…haven't got a hangover?'

'I think I'm old enough and experienced enough to recognise a hangover,' Gabriel said.

'Then it's probably just a bug you picked up. There are a few of those flying around. I'll make sure your meetings are cancelled and you can let me know later in the day if I need to rearrange any of the ones you have booked for tomorrow.'

'You'll have to come here, Rose.'

'I beg your pardon?'

'I'll need you to type some urgent stuff up for me.'

'You can't work if you're ill!'

'You know where I live, don't you?'

'I can't come over to your place, Gabriel!'

'Why not?'

'Because…because I have an awful lot to do here…'

'And I have an awful lot to do here. Get a piece of paper and write down my address. And, for God's sake, don't make the journey by bus. Get a cab. I want you here some time before the end of the week.'

'But…'

'I'm keeping strictly to your work to rule, Rose. I'm not asking you to work to an unusually late hour. I'm asking you to have a change of environment for a couple of hours. Now, have you got that pencil?' Without giving her time to lodge another pointless protest, Gabriel rattled off his address and then repeated it slowly to make sure that she'd taken it down correctly. 'Got it?'

'Yes, but…'

'Should take you half an hour to get here, even with a bit of traffic. So I'll see you by ten. I'll make sure the front door's open so you can just let yourself in.' He could have sworn he heard another *but* rising to the surface when he hung up.

Rose stared at the disconnected phone for a few minutes as she tried to get her thoughts in order. She could hardly believe that Gabriel was ill. Ill enough to have taken a day off work. He was always so ferociously energetic that it was hard to imagine him ever being felled by something as small as a bug. She stared at the piece of paper with his address on it. When she thought about actually going into his house or apartment or flat or whatever he had, somewhere posh in Kensington at any rate, she felt physically faint. But what if he really *was* ill? She couldn't imagine that he would take himself off to the doctor's. Heaven only knew if he *had* one!

Sick foreboding made her gather her things together quickly. Whatever disks she might need, her own laptop which the company provided for her free of charge, bits of post that needed to be checked and letters that required Gabriel's signature. Then she rearranged meetings and liaised with a couple of people in Finance who would have to cover for Gabriel at least for the day. She caught a taxi just as it was stopping to let someone off outside the office block.

Nerves kicked in as soon as she had slammed shut the door behind her and leaned forward to give the cab driver Gabriel's address. She could feel her short-sleeved blouse clinging to her as she tried to push down the window so that some breeze could reach her heated face. The knee-length flared floral skirt, which had promised to keep her cool when it had been hanging in her wardrobe, felt horribly constricting in the back seat of a taxi. Everything clung. Even her hair seemed to cling to her skull, making her wish that she had done the sensible thing and tied it back.

When she looked out of the window, she could see that

everyone was as uncomfortable as she was. Red faces, makeshift fans from bus timetables, handkerchiefs wiping backs of necks.

But at least that was where their discomfort stopped. She focused on the black computer case by her side, which was big enough to contain everything, and tried not to think about walking into his domain. She hoped that the surroundings wouldn't be too imposing and that perhaps his thrusting, overwhelming personality found solace in a cottage-style place.

She was wrong. She knew that the moment the taxi stopped in front of an imposing Victorian townhouse in an exclusive crescent which was distinguished by the sheer volume of expensive cars parked nose to bumper outside. She paid the cab driver and asked for a receipt while scanning the pristine row of houses for anything that might look reassuringly unkempt, but no such luck.

The door, as promised, was unlocked, making her wonder how someone as sharp as Gabriel could be so trusting, but as she glanced over her shoulder she noticed Harry sitting in Gabriel's car on the opposite side of the pavement and waved.

Then she was in his…house. Townhouse, she realised, was too unimaginative a term for the place in which she found herself. The floor was a rich dark wood, interrupted, in the hall, by a stunning blue and red geometrically patterned rug and the cream walls, which should have been bland, were a display case for works of art which *looked* horribly expensive.

Rose resisted the urge to peer into some of the other rooms and instead eyed the staircase dubiously.

'I'm here!'

She jumped as his voice surprised her from behind and she spun around to see him standing in one of the doorways, Or rather, she thought, as her heartbeat quickened to a sick-inducing speed, *lounging indolently. Lounging indolently* in a black silk robe which was loosely tied at the front and which appeared to conceal nothing more than bare skin.

Rose nearly yelped. She knew her eyes were round and startled as she made a conscious effort not to stare at the bare legs with their sprinkling of dark hair, the sliver of bronzed chest visible where the lapels of the robe failed to meet. Was he even wearing *underwear?* she thought.

'I expected you a little sooner. Lock the front door, would you?'

Rose was more than happy to do that. Anything to rescue her from the sight of Gabriel Gessi in very little.

He had disappeared by the time she turned back round and she headed for the room from which he had appeared. Spot on.

Rose walked into a room that was striking not because of its size but because of its décor. Deep, rich blues provided a dramatic backdrop for the parquet floor and walls lined with bookshelves. Impressive sash windows were dressed in layers of cream muslin that fell and pooled on the floor and dominating the room was a desk on which all the modern gadgets had pride of place. The computers, one laptop and one full sized, a fax machine, two telephones. And, against the only wall that was not occupied with bookcases or windows, was a long, low couch in a rich Paisley print, the beauty of which was ruined by the pillow and sheet.

Gabriel, she realised, was lying on said couch and had been watching her with amusement as she gawped at her surroundings.

'Blame my mother and sister,' he said, reclining with his hands folded behind his head. 'I wanted lots of white and just enough furniture to fit the requirements of being habitable. Well, don't just stand there with your mouth open. Sit down!'

'Where?'

'Well, there's only one chair available, isn't there? Unless you want to come and perch on the side of the couch here with me?' He patted the couch invitingly and Rose hurriedly went and sat behind the desk. Ready for action. She even pulled out the stack of letters she had brought with her and began sorting them into order of priority, waiting for him to tell her where he wanted to begin. In the meantime, she would not look at him because all that flesh was doing disastrous things to her nervous system.

'Aren't you going to ask me how I am?'

'I'm sorry…' Rose looked at him, flustered. In her haste to avoid staring at him she had bypassed the usual pleasantries and, of course, he would pick up on that even though he himself avoided them like the plague. 'How are you feeling, Gabriel?'

'Terrible.'

'You don't look too bad,' she risked truthfully.

'That's because I'm putting on a brave face. The fact is I've had a helluva night. Very restless. Tossing and turning.'

Rose swallowed. Her thoughts wandered to Gabriel, in a big king-sized bed, powerful, naked body thrashing about. She felt faint. 'In that case, we should finish things here as quickly as possible so that you can get some sleep! It's the best cure there is! Where do you want to start? I've brought the post. I thought you might like to have a look at it…'

'What I'd really like,' Gabriel said, closing his eyes, 'is something to eat. I know it goes beyond your job specification and it's well within your rights to refuse…but I haven't eaten since…hmm…maybe lunch time yesterday…'

'You got me over here *to cook for you?*'

Gabriel looked at her through half closed eyes and wondered whether he should inform her that that particular tone of voice was not at all attractive. Not when he was supposed to be an invalid and she was supposed to be Florence Nightingale. Anyway, what was wrong with cooking for him? He wasn't asking her to rob a bank! He couldn't count the number of women who had been desperate to get into his kitchen and start weaving some magic with one of his frying pans!

'Forget it,' Gabriel said abruptly. 'I might have known that putting yourself out would be unthinkable. I'll do it myself.' He began levering himself off the couch and Rose reluctantly shook her head.

'What do you want?'

Gabriel flopped back down and fixed amazing, sleepy blue eyes on her. It was steaming hot outside. Her clothes were clinging to her even though it was cool in here. Years ago he had had an overhead fan installed and it had been a brilliant idea, even though it only came into its own very irregularly. On a day like this, though, it was so much better than air-conditioning.

'You look hot.'

'I *am* hot.' Rose raised one hand to bundle her hair into a ponytail so that she could fan her neck. Gabriel wondered if she had any idea how provocative she looked, how the movement of her full breasts was very noticeable in what she happened to be wearing.

'You could always strip off…' he allowed a fractional pause '…and change into something a bit cooler. My sisters have random clothes upstairs in the rooms they use and they're roughly your size. You could borrow something.'

'No!' Rose was horrified. She might have altered her look but underneath she was still the same and was frankly horrified at the thought of stepping into someone else's clothes. Especially when it would involve getting out of her own…in Gabriel's house…while he was in it…

'It was just a thought. As far as I know, all the clothes are clean.'

'I know that. And…thank you for the offer but I'm fine. Now, if you just tell me what you want to eat, I'll see what I can do. A sandwich? Or some fruit?'

'An omelette, I think. And toast. Also some coffee, no… tea. Better in ill health, I believe. With sugar.'

'Oh, hang on. I'll just get my pad so that I can write it all down.'

Gabriel grinned. He had always enjoyed her dry sense of humour even though it had been conspicuously absent over the past few weeks when she had been in her Head Down No Nonsense Rose role.

'Think of it as doing an ill man a good deed.'

'Only if you think of it as taking advantage of a good-natured secretary.' Rose exited the room to the sound of his rich chuckle behind her and followed her nose to the kitchen. Like most houses in London, it wasn't a mansion and she located the kitchen without too much difficulty. It was a wealthy bachelor's paradise. Black granite counter tops, chrome double-fronted fridge-freezer with integral ice-maker, coffee-maker that looked as though you would need a degree in electronics to operate it. Nothing looked as though it had ever been used, which either meant that he was rarely to be found doing anything like cooking in his own kitchen or else he had an extremely efficient cleaner.

The frying pan, finally located, was gleaming. It was almost a crime to use it for something as mundane as preparing food.

It was half an hour before she eventually walked back into the study to find him still reclining on the couch. The black silk robe was revealing even more sinfully muscled chest and Rose cleared her throat meaningfully, giving him time to cover himself up, which he didn't. He just sat up, propping himself against the arm of the sofa, which was a band of wood, giving the item of furniture something of a sleigh bed look, a fact she had only now noticed.

'Smells delicious. Where did you find the tray?'

Rose raised her eyebrows questioningly, although it didn't exactly amaze her that he was fairly clueless as to the contents of his kitchen.

'Tucked away in a groove between two of the cupboards. No one would ever guess that it had been used. Along with everything else in the kitchen.' She placed the tray on his lap and averted her eyes as best she could from the enticing glimpse of hard brown skin.

'I don't do a great deal of cooking,' Gabriel agreed, tucking into the food with evident relish. 'In fact—' he paused to look at her '—the last time I ate home-cooked food was…three months ago when I went back to Italy for a week.'

'You can't eat out *all the time,* Gabriel!' Rose was suitably shocked by the thought of that. 'It's impractical, never mind the expense.'

'Why is it impractical?'

'Because…it just is. It's not nutritious.'

'Do you make an effort to cook for yourself?'

'Yes. Yes, I do. I enjoy cooking. I find it very relaxing.'

'Maybe you could come and cook for me now and again.' He saw the expression on her face and bit back his sudden impatience. 'Just a joke, Rose. There's no need to snatch the nearest bottle of smelling salts in case you pass out from the horror of such a thought.'

'I don't cook very fancy food,' she said, trying to pour a bit of oil on troubled waters. A cooped up Gabriel was a dangerous Gabriel, especially now the boundary lines between them had become frighteningly blurred at the edges. 'Not the kind of food you would enjoy eating.'

'I'm enjoying this.'

'Stop being difficult, Gabriel. You know what I mean.'

'Do you know you are the only woman I have ever allowed to talk to me like that? Aside from my mother. And, of course, my sisters, who see it as their duty to keep me in my place.'

Rose grinned at the thought of anyone trying to keep Gabriel in his place. She missed the thoughtful glint in his eyes as he contemplated her, back in her position of safety behind the desk, which dwarfed her.

'What makes you think that you know the sort of food I enjoy?'

Was it her imagination or was he dragging it out with that breakfast? Normally Gabriel worked on full throttle, barely pausing to draw breath. It was unlike him to call her over urgently, only to engage her in chit-chat.

'I don't know.' Rose shrugged and looked down at her fingers, at the pale pink polish which she had applied the day before. She never used to wear nail polish but she did now and she liked the way it looked and the feminine way it made her feel.

'How are you doing with finding a suitable course? Is that all sorted out now?' Gabriel changed tack as dragging the conversation on to a personal level obviously wasn't going to work.

And why exactly he was engaged in this ridiculous charade was beyond him anyway. He felt as fit as a fiddle but despite that had been unable to fight off the driving desire to have her in his territory, have her see *him* in it. Why? Because curiosity was eating away at him? He would have considered himself above sexual curiosity, but clearly not, considering he had concocted a lame excuse for her to come to his house for no better reason that to play games. On a weekday. When he should have been in meetings. Hell, it wasn't as if he didn't work all the hours God made, he decided, squashing his guilty conscience. He deserved a break now and again. And when was the last time a woman had captured his imagination?

'Oh, yes, I think so.' She went pink and stared harder at her neatly painted nails. In fact, if only he knew that her search for a suitable course had led her into some very interesting waters.

'You *think* so? Shouldn't you have signed up by now?'

'Yes. Yes, I have, as a matter of fact.'

Gabriel's eyes narrowed on her embarrassed face. He could smell concealment a mile off and wondered what it was she was hiding from him. Surely discussing something as boring as a business course did not warrant an air of secrecy. For a few enjoyable seconds he toyed with the notion that perhaps his capable secretary hadn't signed up for a business course at all. Maybe she had signed up for a pole dancing course. Now *that* would bring a guilty tinge to her cheeks.

'And?' he prodded.

'It starts at the beginning of October, but I shall have to have a day off for induction some time in September. I'll let you know when.'

'And that's it?'

'What?'

'The sum total of details you intend to throw out at me?'

'There's nothing else to tell you! If you're that interested, I could always bring in the prospectus.' Gabriel, in the wrong mood, could turn being maddening into an art form and he was doing it now, looking at her in a way that made her stomach flip over, steamrollering his way into her private life even though she had spent weeks giving off all the right Keep Out vibes.

'Shall we crack on with the workload?'

Prepared to face a barrage of questions that she would be obliged to dodge like flying bullets, Rose was momentarily taken aback by his change of tack. But she jumped on the bandwagon gratefully and after half an hour her pulse had settled back down to normal, as had her voice.

He had remained on the couch, seemingly unaffected by the incongruity of conducting work in nothing more than a bathrobe, and she had stayed at his massive desk, typing directly on to the computer, punctuating the pattern with little notes in her pad, which she would research and transcribe back at the office.

She looked at her watch once. The next time she glanced at it, it was lunch time. They had been working solidly for over three hours!

'We'll call it a day now.' Gabriel watched as she flexed her fingers and attempted a stretch. 'Come over here.'

'I beg your pardon?'

'Come over here.'

Rose obediently gathered up her stuff, everything ordered and clipped together neatly so that she could move swiftly through them when she returned to the office.

'Sit.' Gabriel swung his legs to one side and patted a space next to him. 'And don't worry, I won't bite…' There was something softly alluring and very, very feminine about her hesitation. It made a refreshing change from women who were as sexually aggressive as men and didn't need an invitation to get close up and personal.

'I don't want to catch anything.'

'You won't catch anything.' How very true, he thought wryly. 'I'm simply going to massage your shoulders, get rid of some of that tension. Come on. Sit. I'm a very good masseur.'

Rose gasped. Her knuckles whitened as she clutched her

wad of papers with horrified desperation. Was he being *serious? Massage her back?* There was nothing *simple* about the suggestion. Not in her fevered mind. She took a step backwards. She thought she might be overreacting. The amused, self-assured expression lurking on his face was giving her an indication of that, but there was no way that he would be laying a finger on her. She took a couple more steps backwards and of course that was when it happened. Sod's law, she thought, as she grappled and failed to retrieve her footing, that the one place that damned low footstool was, the same footstool he had kicked aside to make way for her and the tray, would be right there behind her left ankle. Just the right spot to ensure that she fell in an undignified heap on to the ground, surrounded by her neatly compiled paperwork and with her flimsy summer skirt in hideous disarray. Rose scrambled to gather herself, her face burning with embarrassment, only belatedly registering that, for someone who was supposedly ill, Gabriel had leapt out from the couch with remarkable agility and was now, horror of horrors, bending over her with a concerned expression, bathrobe agape, allowing her a glimpse of boxer shorts.

Lord, but could things get any worse?

Rose pushed herself up and yanked her skirt down, just as Gabriel scooped her up, ignoring her yelps of dismay. There went the skirt. Riding up. Undoing the job she had just done. Exposing so much thigh that Rose was scared to let her attention linger. And his arms around her were like steel, forcing her head against his chest, bare skin because his robe was in as much disarray as she was.

The whole mortifying episode must have taken all of five seconds, but to Rose, it seemed like eternity. Everything seemed to be happening in slow motion until he had deposited her on the couch, at which point it was real time again except she found that she couldn't jump to her feet, the one thing she wanted to do, because he was kneeling in front of her.

'What *are you doing?*'

'Rotate your foot. That was a pretty bad fall. We need to make sure that you haven't twisted anything.'

'I'm fine.'

'If you hadn't been scuttling off like a little scared rabbit, you would never have tripped.'

Rose wanted to smash him over the head with the nearest heavy object.

'If you hadn't been…'

'Hadn't been what?'

'Do you mind giving me back my foot?' He had removed her shoe and was massaging her foot, working his fingers along the soft underside, rotating it with exquisite pressure until she wanted to scream or groan or *something*. 'Nothing's wrong with it! Everything's fine!'

'Hadn't been what?' Gabriel straightened up, which was a more dangerous position because now he was on her eye level and way too close for comfort. She could so easily slide her hand under his silk robe. Four years' worth of fantasies crashed through her like a tidal wave and Rose closed her eyes briefly.

'Well?'

Rose opened her eyes to find that he was even closer to her. And amused. The smile was right there behind eyes that were pretending to be serious and interested. And here she was, desperately trying to fight down the effect he was having on her. *It just wasn't fair!* Four years fighting off a lethal attraction to a man who had now decided that it might be a bit of fun to flirt with her once in a while, when he was between women and had nothing better to do.

Every fibre in her being regretted the decision she had made to stay put for a while longer.

'If you hadn't been flirting with me,' Rose said coldly. 'If you hadn't forgotten that it's totally inappropriate. I expected more of you.'

She had been hoping to shame him. She failed. He gave her a slow, devastating smile.

'Flirting...' He inclined his head to one side as if considering a new found concept. 'You're right. Maybe flirting was a bad idea. Maybe...' his voice was velvety soft and rich with husky sexuality '...I should have just done this...'

For three seconds time stood still. His mouth touched hers with gentle curiosity, then hungry urgency that had her clinging to him, matching his want with hers in equal measure. And it took ten seconds for sickening reality to intrude.

'Don't!' Rose pushed him so forcefully that he stumbled backwards, giving her time to get to her feet and put some distance between them. 'How *dare you?*'

Gabriel stood up, but he wasn't angry. Not at all. And that was even scarier. The expression on his face was as though he had sorted something out in his head.

'I'll *pretend that never happened,*' Rose gritted. 'But if it happens again, then I'm gone! Do you hear me?' She couldn't bear to look at the discarded shoe, but she did, slipping her foot into it and bending to scoop up all the papers, not caring what order they were in. His silence was unsettling. She knew he was watching her and it made the hairs on the back of her neck rise. Would he see? The way her breasts were still throbbing, aching to be caressed? Or the way the dampness was spreading between her legs, honeyed dew begging for his touch? Rose wanted to die a thousand deaths. She would have remained scrambling around on the floor indefinitely but finally she had gathered up the strewn papers and was looking at him with her best ice cold glare.

'Okay.' Gabriel looked down at her. 'It's a deal. I'll pretend it never happened and you can pretend that you didn't want it to...'

CHAPTER FIVE

THE interviewing was not going according to plan. At least not the plan that Rose had germinated in her head, which basically involved finding someone quickly and installing them even more quickly so that in due time, preferably as soon as she had found her feet on her course, she could re-submit her letter of resignation and this time leave with a clear conscience.

Because Gabriel was driving her crazy. True to her request, he had not mentioned a word about *that kiss* but she had still spent the past week in a state of heightened awareness. Big mistake because she was doubly conscious of him. The minute he got within two feet of her, her entire nervous system went into overdrive and she could feel her body tense in dreaded expectation of some casual physical contact.

Of which there had been a fair few instances. More than usual, although she was pretty sure that she was imagining that. A feathery brush of his fingers on her arm when he leant to read something over her shoulder, the briefest of touches when she handed him a cup of coffee or when he sat next to her so that he could go through some detail with her in one of the reports they happened to be working on. Her antennae now seemed to be on red alert and it was driving her crazy.

Try as she might, her body was not letting her pretend that nothing had happened, even if all mention of it was conscientiously avoided. He came close and she felt faint. He casually touched her and her body roared into hot, suffocating awareness. His challenge a week ago, that he would pretend to forget what had happened if she could pretend that she hadn't wanted it, was proving ominously prescient.

Hence her increasing desperation to find a suitable replacement.

And Gabriel was proving frustratingly uncooperative.

'If this woman is to possibly be your eventual replacement,' he'd told her seriously, 'then I have to make sure that I get it right. We're not talking about someone who's going to be around for a few weeks, someone disposable. I need to find exactly the sort of woman I can happily work alongside…'

'Or man,' Rose had pointed out, but Gabriel had shot her one of those looks that informed her right there and then that working alongside the ideal man was not on the cards for him.

They had thus spent the past three days poring over applications and squeezing in candidates whenever Gabriel had a free moment.

Two women, both of whom seemed to fit the bill, had been rejected out of hand by Gabriel, on the spurious excuse that he *just couldn't see himself having a long and problem-free working relationship with either of them.*

'But it would only be for two days during the week,' Rose had mumbled unconvincingly, because in her head she had already slotted her replacement in on a full-time basis, while she went somewhere else to lick her wounds.

'Would it?' he had asked darkly, and she had given him a weak smile.

Now, at five-thirty, they had just seen off the latest in the ever-increasing line and Rose knew, without doubt, that it had been another unsuccessful interviewee.

She hated this bit, when she walked down to the grand reception area in the foyer and did her best to fend off pointed and anxious questions as to whether the interview had been a success or not. This evening, however, it wasn't too bad. Elaine Forbes, number thirteen in the line, was destined to prove true the superstition because her lightweight qualifications had made the business of rejection easier than usual.

Five minutes debriefing with Gabriel and she would be out of the office and ready to begin her weekend.

She arrived back at her office to find him lounging in her chair, feet propped up on her desk, hands folded behind his head.

'Well?' he asked, picking up her pen and twirling it over, 'what did you think of Ms Forbes?'

'I think we can strike her off the list,' Rose told him, skirting round his indolent figure and gathering her various bits and pieces in preparation for going home. She could feel his eyes following her and hated herself for the excited ripple of reaction. She also hated it when he invaded her space. It was much easier to be in his office, because she could leave it and shut the door behind her. Right now, he was focused fully on her and it was difficult to escape the crazy notion that he was doing it on purpose, because he knew it rattled her. It was a thought that had occurred to her previously during the week and whenever it did she always hastened to tell herself that she was being silly, imagining things because of what had happened between them.

'What makes you say that?' Gabriel asked in a surprised voice and Rose paused to give him a jaundiced glance.

'Oh, I don't know, Gabriel. I guess it might have something to do with her staggering failure to master the basic test I set for her to judge how familiar she was with our computer package. Or maybe her lack of speed and accuracy when it came to taking notes on what I was saying.' Rose knew Gabriel well enough to know that he said most things once and expected immediate comprehension. Floundering was not a quality he appreciated and Elaine Forbes had floundered in a fairly spectacular fashion.

'She was remarkably attractive. Did you notice?'

Rose flushed. Yes, she *had* noticed, as a matter of fact. It would have been hard not to. Five foot ten of curves clad in a handkerchief of a skirt and a top that just skimmed her waistline. Long blonde hair and wide green eyes that had sized Gabriel up and clearly not found him wanting.

'I'm not sure what that has to do with anything.' She fetched her lightweight jacket and slung it over her shoulders. It would still be too warm to put it on when she went outside but old habits died hard. She still felt undressed if she left the house without a jacket or a cardigan. Unlike the most recent candidate, who would probably have felt overdressed in anything as mundane as a cardigan. Or cream lightweight jacket.

'Her credentials weren't up to scratch,' she said irritably, irked at the small smile playing at the corners of his mouth as he obviously contemplated the other assets Ms Forbes would bring to any job.

'Which isn't to say that we might not be able to put her on a course, get her up to speed. Provided her attitude is right...'

'And what...' Rose was in danger of snapping, 'would you qualify as *the right attitude?*'

'An ability to work in perfect harmony with me. That is to say, do whatever I want without complaining.'

Rose narrowed her eyes and was about to ask whether he had a problem with her just because she happened to have lodged a couple of small complaints after *four* years when she realised that he was joking.

'Ha, ha.'

'I admit she might not have the required intellect to hold down the job,' Gabriel conceded, 'despite all her other, highly visible assets.'

Rose was getting tired of being baited. 'I really must be off, Gabriel.'

'Not so fast.'

'Well, there's not much left to say on the subject of Ms Forbes. I'm glad we both agree that the person who fills the position will have to have more going for them than long legs, long hair and breasts.'

'I wasn't about to prolong the conversation about the delectable Ms Forbes. I was going to tell you that there are some emails I need to get out today. The interviewing has thrown everything out of sync. So…you'll have to stay on an extra hour or so until we get the workload covered.' He held up his hands as if defending himself from the possibility of a physical attack. 'And yes, I know it probably crashes through your work to rule barrier but I want to remind you of exactly how generous your pay package is.'

'I don't have a problem working an extra hour or two, Gabriel.' *And he knew it.* 'You *know* that! I only have a problem when you ask me to work ridiculous hours and it really only reared its head because, if I'm going to be studying, I'm going to need to prioritise my spare time!'

Gabriel was beginning to wonder how it was that he had never noticed the feisty, challenging side of his perfect secretary's personality. How could he *ever* have found her *soothing?* She was about as soothing as a shark in search of blood! Fortunately he was man enough to tackle any form of shark. And to enjoy the tussle. Right now he was mightily enjoying the sight of her turning pink as her feathers were well and truly ruffled. He also liked the fact that he got under her skin, that under her carefully cultivated cool exterior, the one that had had him hoodwinked for so long, she responded to him. As a man. He was pretty sure that she hadn't been able to relegate that kiss to the back of her mind and that pleased him because he sure as hell hadn't been able to forget it. Just thinking about her cool lips against his, about that instant, that one fleeting moment, when she had opened up and returned the kiss with a fire she was at pains to hide, was enough to make him feel hard. Like an adolescent in the throes of his first crush.

For Gabriel that was a sensation so novel that it was enough to keep him up at night. He suspected that thoughts of him might well keep her up at night too. With any other woman he would have asked, knowing that it was really a very sexy question, especially if he qualified it by saying that the sleepless nights were mutual, but that was the last thing he would have done with Rose. He had no doubt that she would have flung that damned resignation letter straight at him and this time she would have not been open to persuasion.

But he wanted her and he was pretty sure that she wanted him and he had time on his side. Well, sufficient time anyway.

'Of course I know that! But we still have some work to put in here and I'm glad you don't have a problem.' He stretched and rubbed the back of his neck. 'Now, if you want to come into my office, we can start downloading the files we need to have a look at and you have my word that I won't keep you past the witching hour.'

Not so fast, Rose wanted to shout as he disappeared towards his office.

'I'm afraid there's a bit of a problem with staying on tonight,' she said awkwardly, following him in but standing in the doorway, hands in her jacket pockets.

Gabriel, who was leaning over his desk, booting up his computer in preparation, looked up and frowned.

'I thought we'd sorted that one out,' he said abruptly.

'You don't understand. I can't work tonight because I'm busy…'

'You're busy?'

He sounded truly shocked and Rose knew why. Because in all the four years that she had worked for him, she had rarely denied his requests that she work beyond the call of duty. She had put her job ahead of everything. It satisfied her and coincidentally fed her hidden addiction to him. Over the years he must have gained the impression that she had no social life, nothing to distract her from her complete slavish dedication to *him*.

She felt an illicit thrill of pleasure at bursting the bubble.

'I'm busy,' she repeated with a slight nod. 'I could work late on Monday, if it'll keep till then.'

'It won't *keep till then,*' Gabriel said irritably, giving her his full, undivided attention. 'Things at this level don't *keep* indefinitely, Rose. Business doesn't take time out so that we can all have a bit of a rest.'

This was Gabriel at his most coldly sarcastic. It was the voice he saved for when he was well and truly disgusted. He had not scaled the heights by being kind, considerate and retiring. Yes, he was charming and witty and could promote the illusion of being absolutely relaxed, but beneath the velvet glove was the steel hand.

'Well, Gabriel, I'm afraid there's nothing I can do. If you like, I can see whether Emily's free and doesn't mind working late this evening.'

'I have a better idea. Why don't you just cancel whatever it is you were doing? If you were going out with your girl-friends, tell them, from me, that I'll treat them to an evening out next week, wherever they want to go, no expense spared. Call it compensation for putting you out.'

'I'm not going out with my girlfriends,' Rose said eventually. She could almost see his ears prick up.

'No?'

'No.'

'Then what's so important that you can't cancel…?'

'Really, Gabriel, it's none of your business.' But he would make it his business. She knew that. And she didn't know why she was bothering to resist. It wasn't as though she was hiding some shameful secret.

'I think I deserve a decent excuse…'

'I'm going out on a date, if you must know. To the theatre, actually. To see *Les Miserables.* I've wanted to see that for ages. The tickets are all booked and, really, I have just enough time to make it to the theatre. Then Joe and I are going go have a quick bite afterwards. So you see there's no chance I can stay late. I'm sorry.'

'The theatre? Joe? Who the hell is Joe? A quick bite?'

'I have to go or I'll be late.'

'Who is this Joe character?'

'Have a good weekend and I shall see you on Monday, Gabriel!' With which, Rose fled. Not ostensibly. Not to the extent that she was working up a sweat, but moving quickly enough to put a stop to Gabriel's barrage of questions.

She only breathed a sigh of relief when she was in the taxi and speeding to the theatre, and really, really, only relaxed when she was delivered to the theatre and spotted Joe waving at her through the milling crowds.

This was going to be their first date and Rose teetered between anticipation and apprehension. After all, she didn't know him that well. They had met only a couple of weeks previously, a case of pure coincidence. Rose had gone to see one of the colleges on her list and, having set off in anxious pursuit of the business studies department, had ended up in completely the wrong area and knocking on completely the wrong door.

Fortunately for her, Joe had answered it and he had been so nice and so helpful that Rose had found herself opening up to him and confessing her complete ignorance of the further education system, not to mention her utter confusion at finding herself surrounded by so many students, carrying files and laptops, listening to their iPods and generally making her feel like someone from another era.

She had made sure to go to the college dressed in jeans and trainers, in an attempt to blend in, but even her jeans and trainers seemed to be of just the wrong variety, ever so slightly off-key. Rose had poured it all out over the coffee Joe had insisted on buying her in the college canteen.

In the end she had found the right department but, as it turned out, the course wasn't quite what she wanted. So the college was out but Joe, a friend made, was in.

They had exchanged numbers and from that peculiar meeting had blossomed a growing friendship on the telephone.

Rose wasn't sure what would emerge from the friendship but she was willing to follow the road wherever it might take her.

And the evening was a success. The play was good and, over a very late evening meal, they discussed it amongst a thousand other things. She even found herself telling him about Gabriel! Not about her ridiculous feelings for him, of course, but about his annoying, unpredictable ways. In fact, she had to stop herself or risk becoming a bore, and then they chatted easily about Joe and what he did and, before she knew it, it had gone midnight and he was hailing a cab for her.

'I guess this is the time when I ask whether you'd like to risk my company again,' he said, pulling her to one side and kissing her on the forehead. A perfect end to a lovely evening, Rose thought. No pressure for sex, no pushiness. And he was cute too. Blond hair, blue eyes that crinkled when he smiled, and he smiled a lot.

'I think I could see my way to doing that…' Rose couldn't help but smile back at him. 'It's been a great evening out.'

'And we never even got around to discussing what course you've finally signed up to.'

'Oh, and *that's* the most riveting conversation in the world!'

'Absolutely riveting. Don't forget I'm a lecturer. I like to know what it is that you students are interested in.' He smiled again and turned to open the cab door for her. 'So there's no question now. We have to go on another date. Research purposes for me. I'll give you a call on Monday, first thing. I have no idea how much time I'll have to myself on this outward bound weekend of mine. Does this ogre of a boss allow you to use the land line for personal calls or should I call your mobile?'

'Mobile…' Rose said hurriedly, as a mental picture of Gabriel flashed into her head. 'Definitely mobile.'

'In case he ties you to the typewriter and forces you to type a thousand times…*I must never disobey company rules*…?'

'Oh, no. Gabriel's very fair.' It was fine for her to air her moans but she felt hot and flustered at Joe's slight hint of criticism. 'In fact, there's a very low employee turnover rate. One of the lowest in the city. He would…'

'It was meant to be funny, Rose,' Joe interjected gently. 'Now, off you go, Cinderella, before the taxi decides to leave you behind. I'll call you tomorrow.'

He would. Amongst all his good qualities there was a dependability to Joe that Rose knew was just what every woman wanted. If he said he would call, then he would. He was, she went to bed musing, a thoroughly decent man. Not the sort to string a woman along. Not the sort to equate caring with buying expensive gifts. Not a man given to large, extravagant gestures. Definitely not a man who should carry a *Dangerous to Health* warning on his forehead so that women could take note and keep away. And not a man that would make her skin tremble every time he was near.

But there was a spring in her step when she went to work the following Monday. Joe hadn't called but he had sent her a couple of brief text messages, making her laugh with his outward bound stories which he promised to bore her with more fully when they met.

She arrived to find Gabriel already at his desk and, judging from his rolled up sleeves and lack of tie, he had been there a good while. And he did not seem to be in the best of moods.

Rose decided that she wouldn't allow that to deflate her. She fetched him his coffee before making her way into his office and the smile only wavered when he raised his head and frowned at her.

'I'm pleased to see that one of us had a good weekend.'

'Good morning, Gabriel.' She sat in her usual chair, facing his desk, notepad on her lap, ready to begin the day.

He grunted.

'I've brought you your coffee. Is there anything urgent you need me to do or shall I just crack on with the emails from Friday? Don't forget you've got another two ladies to see this afternoon. I've already had the preliminary interviews with them and both seem promising.'

'Cancel them.'

'What? Why?'

'Because one of our places in the Caribbean is behind with some building work and now there's a hold up on some vital equipment, so we're going to have to try and sort this out before the end of the week, preferably before the end of the day.'

'Why the urgency?' Rose was well aware of which particular development this was. There had been ongoing problems with it from day one. The island was very small and very difficult to access. Supplies, in the first stages of building, had been a nightmare to ship across and things had pretty much carried on with that handicap. Gabriel had mentally written the venture off as an ongoing white elephant. It had lost its appeal as a commercial venture, but she knew from the way he spoke about it that he had developed a peculiar fondness for the place. The original structure of a hotel had gradually morphed into a massive villa overlooking the wild side of the Atlantic and the details were more appropriate to a private residence than to a busy tourist spot. Gabriel now nurtured the plan of turning it into an exclusive fourteen bedroomed villa which would be rented for corporate entertaining or else hired by the super-wealthy for the occasional retreat from the rat race.

'There are murmurs of an approaching hurricane. Eileen's sweeping towards Florida but there's a chance it might divert and if it hits us it's going to be fatal for the project. There just aren't sufficient bricks in place to stave off a category four.'

'I'll see what I can do...' Rose privately thought that there was nothing she could do. Time and urgency meant different things out there. The infrastructure on the island, from everything she read in the files, was basic. There were some shops, a school, transport to and from the island. Business was something that happened offshore, largely.

'Good. And, in the meantime, sort out flights for me to get

there. I'll leave first thing in the morning or today if nothing's available for tomorrow.'

'Leave?' Rose looked at him in astonishment. She could feel the blood seeping out of her face and she cleared her throat briskly. 'Leave as in *travel to an island which is on alert for a hurricane?* Where would you stay when you got there? You've been there, Gabriel, and we've both seen detailed pictures of the place. There are no hotels.'

'I could always camp down on the beach.' He stood up and began prowling his office, deep in thought. As he prowled, Rose tried to imagine Gabriel caught up in a hurricane, at the mercy of the elements. The trip to the island was a convoluted one, involving two airports and a boat crossing. What if the hurricane hit while he was in the boat? He would be as vulnerable as an ant in a matchbox hurtling down a waterfall. She shivered and surfaced from the nightmarish reverie to find that he had stopped in front of her. Before she could take evasive action, he was leaning over her, caging her in, his face dark with anger.

'Wake up, Rose!'

'I'm sorry...' She stuck her chin out defensively and thanked the stars that mind-reading wasn't one of his many talents. If it had been, he wouldn't have had much trouble deciphering the dread inside her as she contemplated the foolhardiness of what he proposed to do.

'You're no use to me mooning about the place,' he snapped, thrusting his face aggressively towards hers.

Rose had no idea what he was talking about but, whatever it was, it was a darn sight safer than being accused of being no use to him because she was worried to death.

'You come to work, Rose, and you leave the love struck business behind in the bedroom!'

Realisation dawned and she opened her mouth to protest but then immediately thought better of it. There had been too much entanglement of her private life with her professional one recently and it was time for her to re-define the boundaries.

'Right,' she agreed readily and was treated to an even more thunderous frown before he pushed himself away and strode back to sit behind his desk.

'Cancel everything in my diary for the week ahead. I don't anticipate being out there longer than a couple of days but there's nothing predictable about the weather.'

'It's a ridiculous plan, Gabriel.'

'Thank you for your opinion. That will be all for the moment.' Somehow it seemed all wrong for his perfect secretary to have spent the night making passionate love to a man she barely knew. Because she hadn't denied it and he knew her well enough by now to know that if she was innocent of the accusation she would have denied it vigorously. Despite the change in her appearance, her sense of morality was too ingrained.

What she got up to or didn't get up to was, he acknowledged, a side issue. There were far bigger problems on his plate for him to give even a passing thought to Rose in the arms of a man, but he was finding it hard to rid himself of the image.

'How was your theatre date on Friday?' he heard himself asking. 'Fun?'

'What?'

'Theatre? Last Friday? You were going to see *Les Miserables*?'

'Oh. Right. Yes, of course. It was brilliant. Thank you.' Rose wondered where the change in conversation was leading and decided that it was probably just his distracted way of taking his mind off the enormous problem of how to tackle several hundred thousand pounds worth of incomplete bricks and mortar that was in imminent danger of being reduced to rubble. In truth, he barely looked as though he was paying her the slightest bit of attention.

It was a learning experience to realise that this was the man whose possible brush with any danger whatsoever was enough to reduce her to a state of witless tension.

'Joe was wonderful company!' she added, more to remind herself that there *were* actually normal, genuine, caring men on the planet, men who were far more worthy of her care and attention than the brooding powerhouse sitting in front of her.

Which means what? Gabriel wondered. The mere fact that he was *wondering* was enough to rouse anger at his own weakness. Unlike most men, he had never personally found women to be an incomprehensible species. On the contrary. The women he had wined, dined and bedded had been as transparent as glass. Rose was of a different genetic make up. One minute she slotted nicely into the pre-packaged box in his head, the next minute she had wriggled out and was proving wrong everything he had thought of her. From capable, controlled, private, inoffensive but slightly frosty secretary to sexy, new style, new look, suddenly ambitious woman with a core of fire, to, apparently, vamp who would sleep happily with a man who barely registered as acquaintance on the *How Well Do I Know You?* chart.

Did she really imagine that he wanted to conduct a conversation about her nobody date when he had important things on his mind?

'Is that female speak for *the perfect gentleman?*' Gabriel asked sneeringly.

'I take it that in the world of Gabriel Gessi, being the *perfect gentleman* is considered something of a crime?' Rose asked, bristling.

'Not a *crime*. Just ever so slightly...*dull*...'

'Joe is anything *but* dull, as a matter of fact...'

'There's no need to sound so defensive, Rose! I believe you! I can't imagine you would ever go out with someone as dull as dishwater. In fact, I can't imagine anyone dull would know how to handle you!'

'I don't need *handling*. I'm not a wild animal.'

'Well, you're not most men's idea of submissive either.'

'I am *not* going to get embroiled in this.' She took a few deep, steadying breaths. Until recently she had been submissive enough. At least on the work front. 'I don't want to discuss Joe.'

'You're the one who brought him up.' Gabriel shrugged. Perfect gentlemen didn't usually seduce their women into bed on date number one. So, whatever it was that had constituted their brilliant evening, it probably hadn't been a vigorous romp in the hay, and that was enough to put him in a better mood. 'But you're right. There are more important things to discuss. When you've sorted out flights and transfers, let me know immediately and also I'll need to have an hour or so with the boys in Finance, just to brief them on a few things they'll need to handle in my absence...'

His attention was already far away from the subject of her and her date. Having chipped in with his uninvited opinions, he had now forgotten the matter and was moving on. Typical. He rattled her cage and, while her teeth were still clattering from the shock, he had disappeared off into the distant horizon, leaving her to gather her untidy, scattered thoughts.

'I still don't know what you think you can do over there if a hurricane *does* strike,' Rose said, standing up and once again focused on the dreadful thought of Gabriel caught up in the elements. 'You might joke about camping on a beach but there's nothing funny about the situation, Gabriel.' Her heart squeezed painfully. 'People die in situations like that and it's just stupid to pull a macho stunt and think you can deal with it.'

'Somebody has to,' Gabriel told her seriously, 'and it's not going to be the foreman on the site. My venture, my responsibility.'

'That is *so* bloody typical of you, Gabriel Gessi!' Rose finally exploded from a combination of sickening fear and sheer frustration. 'You think you can handle anything! That you're invincible and *you're not!*' Tears wanted to spring from the back of her eyes but there was no way that she would allow that level of emotion to seep through. 'It's not a sign of *strength* to never admit to being weak!'

'You're worried about me?'

'Of course I'm worried about you!' And, just in case her response was too dramatic, 'Anyone would be!'

'There's no need,' Gabriel said gently. He itched to go over to where she was standing in tight-lipped silence and hold her close against him. For once, he wasn't finding it claustrophobic to have a woman openly show her concern for him. 'The building may not be complete but what's there should be structurally sound. It's taken long enough but it's been constructed to hold firm against the elements, even though the island doesn't lie in a hurricane path. I shall have a solid roof over my head. Only one wing will be exposed to the elements and even that will stand. I suspect the electricity and water might fail if the hurricane hits but, aside from that, I'll be fine.' He grinned. 'Doesn't everyone long to get close to nature? Now I have my big chance.'

Rose looked at the devilishly handsome face and sighed to herself. She did believe him when he said that the structure was solid but, even if it wasn't, she knew that he would probably have gone to the island anyway. In another life, he would have been a Formula One racing driver, enjoying the challenge of dicing with death.

'Of course if you're *that* worried,' he purred softly, 'you could always come with me. Damn good opportunity to see exactly how much more work needs to be done on the place instead of relying on emails and reports…'

CHAPTER SIX

THE more Gabriel thought about it, the better he liked the idea of Rose accompanying him out to the island. He was utterly convinced that, hurricane or no hurricane, neither of them would be in any physical danger and somehow the thought of having her for company was very appealing.

'We would probably be able to make some serious inroads into sorting out the niggles that have been blighting this whole business for months,' he pointed out. 'And having you around would mean that I could work twice as fast because I wouldn't have to do any of the transcribing myself. Four days and I reckon we could have the matter under control.'

Rose looked at him as if he had suddenly taken leave of his senses. 'You're expecting to *work* while a hurricane rages outside?'

'We don't know that the hurricane is going to hit the island.'

'But the weathermen seem pretty convinced.'

'Weathermen are notoriously wrong when it comes to reporting on the weather. In fact, in any other line of work the sheer inaccuracy of their reporting would get them sacked on the spot.'

Rose opened her mouth to protest at Gabriel's vast sweeping assumption but he was already moving on, developing his plans out loud.

'Of course, I realise that with this course ahead of you and the glittering prospect of a bright new career, you might no longer have the necessary dedication to tackle a job that's going to take you out of the country…'

'You know I would never give anything but one hundred and one per cent to the job!'

'Except when it happens to fall at inconvenient times…'

'There will be no one on the island, anyway,' Rose pointed out dubiously. Her knowledge of the place was pretty sparse, confined to the brief dispatches she had read over the months, but mostly she knew of the hiccups in the nuts and bolts of the building work and little else. 'Who do you plan on talking to about what's been going on with the site if there's no one there?'

'Of course there'll be people there! You don't think they're conveniently going to disappear while there's a hurricane watch on because they all just happen to have second homes somewhere else, do you?'

Rose reddened and glared at him. 'I'll go and sort the flights out.'

'Book two.'

Rose paused by the door and stared him down, which was a very difficult thing to do when her heart was thumping like a steam engine inside her chest. 'I'm afraid I just won't be able to make it, Gabriel…'

Gabriel's eyes narrowed. 'It's not this man, is it? Getting in the way of your job even though he's only been on the scene for two minutes…?'

'Of course not!' At the back of her mind, she knew there was absolutely no imperative to defend her decisions but Gabriel's pointed silence accompanied by that infinitesimal raising of his eyebrows was enough to get every self defensive mechanism in her body rearing up into immediate action.

'Joe would never dream of being chauvinistic enough to try and dictate how I conduct my working life...'

'No. I forgot. He's the perfect gentleman.' Gabriel grinned and got a well-deserved glower in response.

'I can't come with you because...'

'It *would* be incredibly helpful...'

'Because...' Rose ignored his velvety interruption '...there's too much to do here, especially as I've had to take a bit of time out with all the interviewing...' The pointless interviewing, she wanted to add.

'I'm the boss. I'm excusing you for the next four days. There's too much to gain, if you accompany me, in terms of speed...'

'You could take Ralph... Surely someone on the board would be better served there with you...' At this point she had virtually jettisoned the sensible argument of how exactly work would be conducted if they were having to shore up the building with sandbags or whatever. Hard to transcribe emails in gale force winds and twenty foot waves.

'Somehow I don't think Ralph would be overly impressed at having to play secretary to me out there. Anyway, I doubt his ability to type is as quick as yours... I just don't get it, Rose... You've never had a problem accompanying me on trips before...'

'Not to storm-battered islands in the middle of the ocean...'

'Which brings us back to those damned over-pessimistic weathermen. Why don't you book the passages over and if you do decide to come I would be very grateful.'

He returned his attention to whatever was absorbing it on his computer screen and Rose, taking the hint, left his office, shutting the door quietly behind her.

Okay, she would book the two passages. He had given her permission to change her mind. The wasted fare would be peanuts to him. Not only could his conglomerate absorb it but he could personally absorb it as well and not even miss it from his bank account.

Everything was booked for first thing the following morning. She had checked on the Internet and gathered that the likelihood of the hurricane sweeping over the island was fairly remote. They probably would be able to get some vital work done.

She paused at the easy way she had assumed herself to be accompanying him.

So, she didn't want to go but he was right. She had never complained before about going with him to meetings, over-nighting in the same hotel as him. If she made a point of com-plaining now and refusing to go, his sly little brain would soon start whirring into action and he would either mistakenly assume that she had morphed into a bimbo whose private life was influencing her professional one or, worse, he would think that she was scared to be in his company.

In the very dark recesses of her mind crept another taboo thought. The notion that the weather might defy the odds and she knew, deep down, that if he was to find himself in any trouble she would want to be by his side.

Where that left Joe, perfect gentleman and epitome of ev-erything a mother would like her daughter to bring home, was a question she would deal with later.

Four days wasn't long and it might well be less, depend-ing on circumstances.

It was what she told herself the following morning as she slung clothes into her pull-along suitcase. Neither of them were taking anything that would have to go into the hold. Too much opportunity with the various changes en route for it to go missing in action. Gabriel would also be bringing his laptop computer, although whether they would be able to link up to a phone line was anybody's guess.

In any event, Rose packed notebooks and pens. The old-fashioned tools were often the best under pressure.

Work kept them busy for the better part of the flight to one of the bigger islands. Rose read the reports at a furious pace. Together they discussed what could be done to shore up the naked part of the site if bad weather struck. When they weren't working, Rose feigned sleep. And then the tail-end of the journey was lost in the confusion of changing planes and finally taking a boat over with the boat man reminding them constantly that they were mad to be undertaking a trip when the weather was going to change. Hurricanes rarely affected that particular spot and the man seemed unnaturally enthusiastic about the possibility of one.

By the time they finally hit their destination, Rose was practically dead on her feet. She had started the day at a little before five and had had very little to eat.

Nightfall on the island, in conjunction with very few street lights, meant that she could barely appreciate the scenery. Not that it made much difference when all she wanted to do in the back of the prehistoric taxi as it bumped its way over the single track road was to nod off and go to sleep.

How did Gabriel manage to keep going for so long without any signs of wear and tear? He didn't even look grubby! Maybe because he had chosen his clothes cleverly.

He was saying something to her now and, in reply, Rose yawned widely.

'Not the kind of response I usually evoke in a woman,' he murmured, to which she yawned again and he patted his shoulder, an irresistible invitation for her to rest her head on it. Which she would, she decided. Just for a minute or two, until she became accustomed to the sticky heat which was quite different from the soaring summer temperatures in England.

She awoke to the sensation of the clanking car shuddering to a halt and her eyes flew open.

Horror of horrors, she'd dribbled! There was a damp patch on his shoulder and when their eyes met, he shot her a crooked smile.

'Don't worry. It's human.'

Rose pretended to misunderstand. 'What is?'

'I actually found it quite sweet, somehow innocent, for you to be resting your head on my shoulder and dribbling ever so slightly.'

Rose's mortification followed her out of the car but, as soon as she gazed at the work in progress in front of her, every hesitant self-conscious emotion fell away.

She was staring at something so ambitious and so impressive, even in its half-finished state, that she gasped aloud.

'Like it?' Gabriel was just behind her, bending down to murmur the question into her ear.

'There's still a way to go,' she said prosaically.

'Coward. Why don't you just admit that you love it? It's an architectural adventure.'

'Who designed it?'

'I did.'

'You?'

'No need to look so shocked.' Gabriel lightly ushered her in with his hand under her elbow. 'You're not the only one with a few secrets up your sleeve.'

Rose was too stunned by what she was seeing to argue the toss with him.

The original gloriously opulent hotel with its sprawling network of state-of-the-art condos, which had been the original plan and which, in fact, was still accessible on the computer, along with all the other documents, had been transformed into what appeared to be three dwellings, either very close together or else linked in some way. Each had its own individual turret and encircling them was a broad patio, still in its primary stage but which, he was telling her, would eventually be weatherproof hardwood.

The land which had originally been intended for the condos would become a nine hole golf course—a very challenging nine hold course, he hastened to add, not for the faint-hearted. A short but killer links course, benefiting from the sea breeze that blew along the coastline.

Right at the moment, the sea breeze was still gentle, although the driver had told them that people had already started leaving the island if they could and, if they couldn't, they were battening down the hatches and preparing for the worst, getting tinned food and bottled water in for the duration.

Rose anxiously tried to work out how secure the structure would be in a raging hurricane. It looked pretty solid and almost completely finished in terms of its final build but, since she had no idea about foundations, she couldn't say for sure.

'Anything that can move has been stowed away safely,' Gabriel said, reading the direction of her concern. 'If the worst comes to the worst, there won't be any flying benches or planks of wood.'

'The sky's so blue…it's hard to think that a hurricane might be on the way.'

'I know, but in this part of the world the weather can change in a matter of minutes. Isn't that right, Junior?'

Junior, the driver, was at least seventy. A very sprightly and knowledgeable seventy. They entered the building to a long, informative monologue on the weather patterns of the Caribbean.

Rose was the first to stop and stare. The façade had been impressive enough, but inside was a fertile imagination in full flight. She had expected square, unfinished brick and cement buildings, maybe with the occasional homage to detail that would distinguish them from the run of the mill. Not so. Black and white tiles were the backdrop for a dramatic water feature that dominated the far corner of the entrance hall. The rooms on the ground floor, Gabriel was explaining to a speechless Rose, would be dedicated to the kitchens, the restaurant and all the various domestic necessities that made a place run efficiently, including a health spa. The floor above housed some of the bedrooms and sitting rooms which could be used by the guests at any time of the day or night. The feeling would be one of a home away from home.

'I don't know anyone who has a home like this,' Rose murmured, taking in the detail in the woodwork and the artistry in the way the place had been designed. 'You thought of this *yourself?*'

'I'm a frustrated architect,' Gabriel said lightly, but when Rose glanced across at him he wasn't grinning. 'Leave the bags, Junior, and you head back to your house. Start packing the corned beef away.' He grinned at Junior, who launched into a protest that was swept aside. 'We've got food. We've got drink. We'll be fine. You can come out when the worst is over.'

Rose was dimly aware of this exchange of conversation as she ventured further into the villa, noting that it was in a far more advanced state of completion than she had expected. So much for her fears for Gabriel as he hunkered down in a building with no roof, missing walls and absent plumbing, at the mercy of the unforgiving elements.

At least here everything was finished. The tiled lobby led through to splendid wooden floors, the windows were beautifully dressed with colonial-style shutters, there was paint on the walls and ceilings. All that seemed to be missing was the water from the water feature that spanned one corner of the entrance hall and the prerequisite plants.

'I had no idea the place was fully operational!' Rose said accusingly. 'Where's Junior?'

'Gone to take care of his family.'

Which just left the two of them. Alone. In the urgency of the travel plans and the hectic nature of the trip, Rose had not paused to contemplate in any real depth what the situation would be when they finally made it to their destination. She'd assumed, in her naïveté, that the hotel would be uninhabitable and they would therefore book into whatever inn was available. But the villa was inhabitable, minus anyone else in it. Her heart slowed and for a few seconds she felt giddy.

'He would have stayed. In fact, he would have brought his wife and three of his daughters to take care of us but that really wouldn't have been fair, would it?'

'Of course not.' Lots of empty rooms and just the two of them. Sharing a meal. Waiting for the impending storm. What if the current failed, as it undoubtedly would? She had visions of the two of them, huddled in a dark room with just one another for company. Not an ideal situation for safe, casual chit chat about work. The giddy spell threatened to become full-blown.

'We'd better go and check the kitchens, see what's there and then we'll sort out sleeping arrangements.'

Outside, Rose could hear the sound of the surf and the little noises of night creatures going about their business. It reminded her of Australia, which was a depressing thought because that in turn reminded her of the fact that she shouldn't be here with Gabriel because, actually, she should have left his employ to seek greener pastures elsewhere.

He was already striding off and Rose hastily followed. She felt tired and hot from the long trip but a shower would come later. A shower and a long rest so that she could recharge her batteries for whatever lay ahead the following day.

They passed through various rooms, all in a state of virtual completion.

'I thought you said that there was a lot of work still to be done, that you needed to be here just in case something happened to the structure if the hurricane struck?'

They had finally arrived at the kitchens, which were equipped but in a basic fashion. There was a fridge, obviously one used by the workforce when they were in the villa, and various other cooking utensils, all bearing the signs of use. No oven but something portable on which to cook very simple meals. A table of sorts.

'All this will go, eventually.' He went to the fridge, pulled it open and was pleased to see some perishables, including cheese, eggs and butter. He knew what would be in the cupboards because he had spoken to the foreman as soon as he had decided to go to the island and had instructed him to stock up. Of course, at the time, he had not known that Rose would be with him.

Gabriel was still slightly surprised that she *was* there, although he knew why. Despite her show of laying down laws, Rose was a perfectionist who was deeply devoted to her job. It was simply the way she was built and he admired her for it. Whatever she did, she would do wholeheartedly. He had appealed to her Achilles heel, namely her sense of duty in sorting out what had been a thorny problem for both of them for a very long time. The villa had had its fair share of setbacks and she couldn't resist his plea to accompany him to the island so that they could sort things out. Unlike most other women, actually *all* the other women he had ever known, the fact that a hurricane might rear its ugly head would not have put her off. She wasn't easily spooked.

And she looked bloody amazing considering she had spent most of the day in various forms of travel, not all of them comfortable. The hair which had started out loose was now dragged back into a pony-tail that was in the process of un-ravelling but still managed to look sexy and she couldn't have been wearing make-up because her face looked as scrubbed as it had before they started the trip. She was also sweetly disgruntled. And probably hungry.

'What will?' Rose gave him a sulky look and wanted to tell him that she didn't really care, at least not at that precise moment in time.

'You're hungry.'

'No, I'm not. I'm fine.'

'Don't be a martyr, Rose. There's nothing more annoying.'

'Oh, right. I've travelled halfway across the Atlantic because I *thought* you needed me to help you sort out this place and suddenly I'm being a *martyr* and getting on your nerves.'

'I'm going to fix you something to eat and you're going to say *thank you* very sweetly and stop being defensive.'

'All *what* will go…?' Rose asked grudgingly, as she watched Gabriel take cans and packets out of cupboards. Fair's fair, she thought. *She* had cooked for him once and so he could jolly well return the favour, especially considering he had manoeuvred her over here on false pretences.

Gabriel glanced over his shoulder at her and, not for the first time since they had left England, Rose wondered how it was that he could manage to look so fantastic after hours of travel. He wore what looked like linen trousers of some indeterminate colour and, although they were creased, they looked *expensively* and *tastefully* creased, and the dark shirt similarly looked *tastefully* dishevelled. Frankly, it was irritating. Especially when she felt like something the cat dragged in.

'These makeshift appliances.'

'I thought you were building a hotel here, Gabriel. I had no idea you had changed the spec.'

'It is still a hotel. Of sorts. A hotel on a far more personal scale than was originally intended.'

'There's nothing on the computer…'

'You probably haven't caught up with all the paperwork. This place is no longer under the umbrella of the company. It's now my personal baby, so to speak.'

'Your personal baby?'

'Of course, it will still remain a rentable option, but that won't be its primary function.'

'You got me over here on a project that has *nothing to do with work?'*

'You chose to come over.'

For someone whose kitchen was full of the latest in high-tech gadgets, he seemed very adept at making do with the basics and was concocting something on the makeshift stove that smelled very good even though it was the product of some cans and a packet of pasta.

Rose realised that he had broken off what he was doing to look at her and she flushed. 'I thought you needed me on a work level.'

'I do. Things still need to be sorted out here.'

'But it has nothing to do with *work.'*

'What's the use in nit-picking, Rose? There are no planes leaving in a hurry. The bottom line is you're here and labouring over whether you should or shouldn't be is a complete waste of time. When we get back to London, I'll make sure to compensate you financially.'

'It's not about the money,' Rose said stubbornly, but now she felt petty and small-minded. And who was she kidding, anyway? She was curious and interested to see the place he had decided to adopt as his own, curious and interested to have that little bit more insight into the man he was.

'Oh, for God's sake.' Gabriel raked his fingers through his hair in pure exasperation. 'Why don't you try taking a little responsibility here, Rose? You knew the plans had been altered. I assumed you'd read the financial reports and worked out that the whole project had been transferred out of the company and into my own private banking.'

'I…' *Skimmed over the financial report.* She had expected something and so hadn't checked to see if things had altered on that front. 'Oh, you're right. I'm here now. So why don't you fill me in on what made you change your mind about…the purpose of this place…?' Amongst his network of other financial concerns, Gabriel owned a small but elite chain of hotels in offbeat places. This island was perfectly suited for the purpose. Out of the way, not a tourist in sight, small enough to be exquisite but not so small that amenities taken for granted were absent. Tourists, Rose had discovered over years of dealing with their complaints, liked quaint, which was a lot different from uncomfortable. Quaint was the overhead fan with the air-conditioning option, as opposed to a stand up fan with open windows for added breeze.

'I got involved with the project, simple as that.' He brought over two plates of food. Pasta, some sort of tomato sauce smothered in cheese, chunks of bread, butter. It smelled delicious and, when Rose hungrily tucked into it, tasted as good as it smelled.

'You get involved with *all* your projects,' she pointed out. 'This tastes great, by the way.'

'Glad you think so,' Gabriel said dryly. 'Appreciate it, though. I don't make a habit of cooking for women.'

Rose thought that that was stating the glaringly obvious. Home-cooked meals were on a par with domesticity and domesticity was not something he liked his girlfriends to experience. Fun, yes. Excitement, yes. Domesticity, absolutely no way.

'You were telling me why you changed your mind on this project.'

'We ran into problems about two months ago with the design. I sacked the architect working on it and decided to give it a go myself.'

'Because you're a qualified architect?'

'Because I...' Gabriel looked at her, fork in one hand.

'Because you...?' Rose's gaze was curious.

'I have a degree in engineering.' Gabriel shrugged. 'And art was always something I rather...liked... Or is that not a very macho admission...?'

'It's an extremely macho admission.' Rose could feel her mouth go dry as their eyes met. 'Don't you know that there's nothing sexier than a sensitive man?'

'Is that your way of telling me that you find me sexy?'

'It's my way of saying that art is a wonderful thing to be interested in.' She could feel herself perspiring as his eyes roamed over her flushed face. 'I...I know you like art. I just never realised that you enjoyed it in a practical manner...'

'Art was one of my A levels. Along with maths, French and physics.'

'So you could have been a painter...'

'Not quite.' Gabriel shot her a crooked smile. 'I lacked the creativity, but combined with my maths, and later my engineering degree, I discovered it could be quite practical when it came to design. Of course, there was no place for that in the world of corporate business, but it certainly came into its own when I sacked Jones from this project.'

Rose hadn't realised that she had finished eating until Gabriel rose and took the plate from her, ordering her to sit down while he tidied. After all, he pointed out, she was there out of the goodness of her heart.

'So all of this…is your creation?'

'Most of it. What do you think?'

'Well, I suppose we all need to do something in our spare time,' Rose said prosaically as he seemed in danger of letting her interest go straight to his already oversized ego. 'Tell me about it.'

Rose forgot that she was hot, tired and sticky. Gabriel cleared away the dishes while she sat at the table and hung on to his every word. By the time he had made her a cup of coffee, with long life milk because there was no fresh milk on the island, she was living his dream for the project, wanted to see it eventually as a sprawling ranch-style villa that could accommodate all the members of his extended family, and the rest.

She wanted to ask whether his vision included his own family and kids, but that would have been a question too far.

'Tomorrow's a big day,' Gabriel said in conclusion, after Rose had bombarded him with every question under the sun. 'If the hurricane's going to strike, it'll strike within the next twenty-four hours. We should both think about getting some sleep.'

Rose felt stiff when she stood up. 'I shall need to have a wash or a shower. Is everything plumbed in?'

'Plumbed in and raring to go. As I said, the hold-ups have been irritating and lengthy but the basics are in, which is a blessing.'

He had advised her to bring her own towel, which she thankfully had, and her own soap. Also lots of mosquito repellent. There were no beds, just mattresses on the ground, which had been brought in specially for them. The workmen would use them afterwards, Gabriel assured her, so they wouldn't go to waste. And there was also electricity, although he warned her to expect nothing if the hurricane struck the following day. For good measure, candles had been provided.

After this short speech Rose wasn't quite sure what to expect, but the room he led her to was more than adequate. No furniture, but large and airy with an enormous *en suite* bathroom attached to it. As with the rest of the place, barring the entrance hall, the floor was of rich wood. There was even emulsion on the walls and shutters on the French windows that led directly on to the outside porch.

'When it's up and running,' Gabriel explained, 'there will be hammocks here and there on the porch so that people can relax out of the sun but still in the fresh air.'

'Your idea?'

'With a little input from my sisters, who claim to need relaxation more than me as they have children.' He walked into the bathroom and gave it the once over. 'There's no mosquito net,' he told her, lounging against the wall, 'and no air-conditioning, so watch out for insects. You can burn one of those coils—' he nodded in the direction of the ground by the bathroom '—but they're not one hundred per cent effective. My advice is to sleep with the French windows shut. Just leave a crack in the windows open to allow a through draught and you can leave the door open as well. You won't die of the heat. It cools nicely at night. I'll be up early tomorrow. I'll wake you. You'll probably be tired but we might need to start securing things and getting prepared for the worst.'

'Right.'

'Are you scared?'

'Of what?'

'Creepy crawlies? Night time in a foreign place? The threat of a hurricane?'

Rose shrugged and shook her head. Nothing was as threatening as what she felt in the presence of the man leaning indolently against the wall in front of her. The strangeness of the situation was as nothing compared to the sudden, terrifying knowledge that they were alone in this place.

'Brave lady,' Gabriel murmured and Rose thought she could detect an edge of sarcasm in his voice.

'Not every woman likes playing the damsel in distress.'

'Most don't have to,' Gabriel commented wryly. 'They naturally freak out at the thought of insects and thunder storms... Well...' he pushed himself from the wall and strolled past her '...good night. If you need anything...you know where I am...in the room next door...'

'Thanks, I won't.'

And she would make sure to lock the door, just in case he got it into his head that she was really a damsel in distress underneath it all, that she really needed him to check on her to make sure she wasn't cowering under the sheet in fear of the mosquitoes. He felt guilty, she suspected, at dragging her here under false pretences, whatever he said about the fact that she should have known the situation, and guilt might well make a gentleman of him.

She locked the door and then locked the bathroom door as well, although her shower was quick and cold. The plumbing might be up and running but it wasn't a comfortable experience, although she did feel clean and refreshed afterwards.

She had to stick her wet towel half out of the bathroom window to dry naturally, as towel rails had not yet been fitted, and the ground was wet due to the lack of a door on the cubicle. But the mattress, basic though it was, was comfortable and through the open window the sounds of night-life were oddly soporific.

Rose fell asleep quickly. When she woke up, abruptly, with the prickling sensation that something wasn't quite right, it took her a few seconds to orient herself and make sense of her surroundings, and then it occurred to her exactly what was wrong.

CHAPTER SEVEN

WHAT woke Rose was the stillness. The night sounds, she realised after a few unsettling seconds, had disappeared. Living in London had acclimatised her to a certain amount of noise at night and its absence was eerie.

She stood up. She felt remarkably okay, considering bed had been a mattress on the floor. No aches and pains anywhere.

She drew back the shutters and opened the window. Now the silence was deafening. As was the lack of movement. No breeze. Nothing. Rose shivered and wondered uncertainly what she should do. Wake Gabriel? She knew nothing about hurricanes. She might be spooked but what if this was just a feature of the tropics? Lots of noise between six-thirty and midnight and then at—she picked up her watch which she had adjusted on the plane and stuck it on—it was a little after three in the morning—at a little after three in the morning the comforting noises gave way to complete silence.

Without bothering to think about it, Rose stuck on a pair of jeans, one of two pairs she had packed, leaving on the baggy T-shirt she had brought to sleep in. Somehow it seemed urgent that she get to Gabriel, wake him up, even if his response might just be to laugh at her and tell her to go back to sleep.

His door wasn't locked. In fact, it was ajar and Rose pushed it open to see him sprawled in slumber on the mattress on the ground. This would be the only time she would ever get to catch him off guard and she couldn't resist the opportunity. She forgot the elemental fear that had propelled her into his room and tiptoed to stand over him. Awake, he was compulsively fascinating, with his high octane energy and sinful good looks, and asleep he was no less so. The sheet covered most of him but he had obviously felt the heat during the night and worked his way free of some of the covering so that part of one leg was exposed and most of his upper body.

Rose licked her lips nervously, unable to break the spell as she stared down at his, quite frankly, perfect body. He looked very brown against the white sheets. His chest was broad and muscular and the dark hair was almost a little too masculine for her curious eyes. She gulped and looked away, but all that did was bring her gaze into contact with one leg, also muscular, also with that disturbingly masculine dark hair. She decided right there and then that waking him up was out of the question. She would sidle off quietly and her fear would gradually ease off. She was about to turn away when he spoke. Just like that. His voice ever so slightly amused.

'Are you finished staring or would you like a bit longer?'

Rose nearly teetered backwards in shock.

'I…I *thought* you were asleep!' She managed to make it sound as though he had purposefully tricked her into staring at him.

'I was. Until you came in. What's the matter?' He began sitting up, which was a bit of a disaster because more of his body was exposed to her carefully averted, yet still fully aware, gaze.

'I…I know this is going to sound stupid, but I…I couldn't hear anything and I got a little nervous.'

'What do you mean, *you couldn't hear anything?*'

'Outside. No noise. It's spooky.' Rose laughed nervously. 'I know you're just going to tell me to get back to sleep...'

'What I *am* going to tell you is that you need to look away right about now if you don't want to see more of me than you might have bargained for...' He yanked back the sheet a fraction of a second before Rose could avert her startled eyes. It was long enough for her to realise that he wasn't wearing the pair of polite boxer shorts she had expected. He wasn't wearing a stitch. She gave a little yelp and stepped back just as he levered himself up.

She knew that he was saying something to her, something about hurricanes and their behaviour patterns, but all her mind could focus on was the fact that less than five feet away her very sexy boss was dragging on some trousers while she stood with her back to him and tried hard not to imagine what she would see if she turned around.

'...so we need to go outside and check everything,' she heard him finish up. 'Of course, you can stay put in here but two pairs of hands and eyes would be a damn sight more helpful than one...'

Slowly her fuzzy brain clunked back into gear and she looked at him worriedly. 'What are you saying?'

'I thought I'd just made it clear.' Gabriel paused to look at her as he pulled on a T-shirt. He was still getting over the pleasant sensation of knowing that she was staring at him. It had been crazily sexy. And now she was looking at him, all wide-eyed and feminine, after his quip the night before when she had told him in no uncertain terms that she didn't enjoy playing the damsel in distress. He was very tempted to remind her of her statement but he thought that that might have been pushing his luck too far.

Uppermost in his mind was the fact that they had to go and do the checks which he had anticipated doing during daylight hours. Nevertheless he couldn't stop his eyes from straying just that little bit, noticing that her T-shirt, baggy though it was, still revealed the glaring fact that she wasn't wearing a bra.

'The calm before the storm...' He headed for the door and she followed, even more spooked by the fact that he actually looked concerned. Gabriel was not a man to be easily rattled. But he was moving quickly now, switching on the lights in the house, warning her that the luxury of electricity might not be with them for too long.

'We'll circle the place together,' he told her, pausing only once when they were outside so that he could look around him, as though judging the gravity of the situation from telltale signs she was not aware of. 'There should be nothing to retrieve, but you can never tell.'

Rose shivered at the tone of his voice and edged a little closer to him.

With no cooling effect from the sea breeze, it was muggy outside and very dark. The lights inside the sprawling house illuminated a small patch just outside the double-fronted doors which led out to the gardens overlooking the sea, but beyond that was inky-black, scarily black. Rose had never seen anything quite like it. She was accustomed to a certain amount of light pollution that came from living in London. Just as she was accustomed to the constant low level noise.

'It's going to happen, isn't it?'

'You don't have to whisper.' He had brought two torches. She had no idea when he had grabbed those, but they were invaluable now as they fanned them along the walls of the villa, both of them moving quickly and finding, to Gabriel's satisfaction, that everything was as it should be.

'Right. Now, inside.' They had covered the outside in a little under forty minutes. 'There's no phone link here yet so I won't be able to check on the Internet for any updates with the weather patterns, but we'll fill some buckets with water and cover them. Come in handy for having a wash in the morning. We'll also start lighting some oil lamps and candles, but no candles where they can be a fire hazard. Think you can manage?'

Rose wondered what he would do if she said *no*. He hadn't brought her over here to look after her. First and foremost, she was his practical secretary, after all!

'Think so!' she assured him briskly.

'Good girl.'

They hadn't made it back to the front doors when the eerie stillness was broken dramatically by a flash of lightning that forked across the sky and was accompanied almost immediately by a clap of thunder that was loud enough to make her ears ring. And then an ominous sound that grew louder as they ran towards the house, hampered by the fact that they had to dodge the usual building debris that was neatly stacked but still an impediment to a clear path.

'Rain!' Gabriel shouted just as it came, in one gusty, raging downpour that was accompanied by the howl of winds gathering speed.

Rose had never experienced anything like it. In under thirty seconds she was drenched. When she looked to her left, she could see the palm trees bending as though some powerful force was trying hard to suck them out of the ground. She had to battle not to be blown backwards.

They slammed shut the door behind them as soon as they were in the safety of the house, and then Gabriel was moving quickly and purposefully, knowing exactly where to go to find the oil lamps. He had obviously given very detailed instructions to the foreman before they'd travelled over and that didn't surprise Rose. He would have considered everything.

'I know you're probably uncomfortable in those wet things, but let's sort out the lamps here and then we can both go and change.'

Even though his attention was elsewhere, Rose was still horribly aware of the T-shirt clinging to her body, outlining her breasts and leaving nothing to the imagination. She surreptitiously tried to flap it into good behaviour but no chance and she couldn't possibly skulk off to change, not when they were clearly facing an emergency situation that needed all hands on deck.

So she did as she was instructed and tried not to stare down at her soaked body and the way her breasts were visible and bouncing under the fine cotton.

From outside came the terrifying sound of strong winds battering at the walls and the distant noises of objects being hurled around outside, obviously things they had missed in their inspection of the grounds.

She was beginning to feel cold in the wet clothes and she had to make a big effort not to let her teeth chatter. Visions of the sea rising up the incline in one ferocious tidal wave did nothing to calm her jittery nerves.

In a God-given stroke of luck, they had finished lighting the last of four oil lamps when the electricity went, leaving them in total darkness save for the watery light from the lamps.

'Right.' Gabriel handed her two of the oil lamps. 'At least these are lit and there are candles in the bedrooms, although these should do for the moment. You okay?'

No. 'Fine. I'm a dab hand at crisis situations like this!'

In the darkness, she was aware of Gabriel grinning at her. 'When all else fails, a sense of humour is all a person needs to keep going. Keep it up!'

'I'll try but I was never good at being a mascot.'

They had found themselves back in the bedroom. Hers.

'You'll need to change and then we should bunk down in one room. Just in case.'

'Just in case what?'

'Just in case this bad weather really kicks in. A strong hurricane can take the roof off a building, although we shouldn't be in too much danger here. But better safe than sorry. If the situation deteriorates, I don't want to have to come looking for you.'

Rose acquiesced quickly. She certainly didn't want to be on her own just now.

'I'll be in with you in a minute. As soon as I've changed.'

She did. Quickly. Into her other remaining pair of jeans and a cotton T-shirt, with her bra safely underneath. Her wet clothes she laid carefully out on the floor although she didn't rate the chances of them drying in a hurry.

The wind was managing to find all sorts of cracks and crevices and the noise was incredible. She almost expected it to sweep through the walls and lift her off her feet, but of course she was safe from that. Even so, it was a relief when she was standing outside Gabriel's room, banging on the door to warn him that she was coming in, relieved to find that he, too, had changed, although into boxer shorts and a T-shirt.

'You're going to be comfortable trying to sleep in *that* getup?'

'I'll be fine! Shall we get my mattress in?'

'Give me a minute.'

Literally a minute and back he was, having hauled her single mattress into his room and plopped it alongside his.

Now, suddenly, the comforting presence of another body next to hers when the whole world outside seemed to be going mad, didn't seem like quite such a brilliant idea.

'You look green,' Gabriel said. 'Don't worry. The building won't collapse around our ears. You forget that I've overseen everything from the foundations to where the walls go, and that I know quite a bit about the structure of buildings and what makes them solid.'

Rose was quietly relieved that he had misinterpreted her sick look. She was also heartily relieved that the only lighting in the room was from two oil lamps, the other two having been dimmed to their lowest level and placed in the bathroom.

'Do you want anything to eat?' he asked, interrupting the disastrous train of her thoughts and she shook her head.

'Okay. In that case, you definitely need something to drink. Wait here.'

He didn't give her time to argue, not that she was going to. She could feel exhaustion creeping over her, but the sickening anticipation of lying down next to him was a more powerful force and promised to keep her eyes wide open for what remained of the night. She didn't make a habit of drinking but she sure as hell figured that there couldn't be a better time for a glass or two of whatever he managed to rustle up.

It was dark rum. And soda water, both of which were in plentiful supply. The workmen weren't allowed to drink on the premises, he told her, but he doubted that held true when they slept there most nights. He had brought the bottle in along with six plastic bottles of soda water and two glasses.

It tasted great. She drank the first one quickly and the effects were pleasantly immediate. Her nerves were beginning to do a disappearing act. In fact, after her second drink, it felt fine to be sitting cross-legged on the mattress, facing him, chatting about their experiences of being caught up in bad weather. Since Rose had precious little, most of the chat came from him and she was more than happy to listen to him as he talked to her. The deluge clattering down against the walls and on the roof and the angry roar of the wind as it gusted along the coastline were a lot easier to bear after some alcohol.

Eventually, Rose yawned.

'Sleepy?'

'Suddenly.'

'You'll never get to sleep in those jeans, you know, and as soon as you do, you'll wake up because you'll be too hot.' He fiddled with the base of the oil lamp and dimmed it so that the room was plunged into near darkness. He had slipped under the sheet, his own sheet, and Rose felt safely tucked away from him.

'And as soon as you realise you're hot, you'll also realise that they're not quite loose enough to allow you to breathe easily and then you'll spend tomorrow feeling like hell because you've had a sleepless night.' He yawned widely and rolled over on to his side with his back to her, leaving her to ponder, in a very unfocused manner, his words of advice.

She waited a while, thinking that, yes, the jeans *did* feel very tight, now that he had mentioned it. It also felt ridiculous to be trying to sleep fully clothed. It was a psychological thing, of course, but once she got it into her head that she was uncomfortable, she couldn't rid herself of the notion that she wouldn't get a wink of sleep unless she took the damned trousers off.

So she did, as unobtrusively as she could. And, while she was at it, she also removed her bra and breathed a little sigh of relief. Both items she placed very carefully next to the mattress, within easy reach for when she got up to stick them back on.

Gabriel, she could tell, was already asleep. She could see it in the rhythmic rise and fall of his shoulders, and her own eyelids were beginning to droop.

The alcohol was working on her like an anaesthetic. She could almost physically feel it drugging her into slumber and then she was gone.

Peace lasted all of an hour and a half. Then came her need to go to the bathroom, something she had failed to take into consideration when she had been happily allowing the rum and sodas to relax her.

The wind was still howling. Rose was tempted to grope her way to the window and peep outside, just to see what was going on, but that would risk waking Gabriel, which was something she intended to avoid.

So she made do with going to the toilet then, with just the flickering light from the oil lamp, her wandering eyes fastened on the one thing she didn't want to see. Right there above the door was something the size of a small saucer, and it was alive. Motionless but alive. And hairy. The sound of the storm outside was nothing compared to the pounding of her heart. Could spiders *smell* fear? she wondered. Like sharks?

She washed her hands. Then, and she didn't know how she managed to achieve this, she tiptoed across to the door, one eye on the spider, the other on her flight path, yanked it open and literally leapt on to the mattress, colliding with Gabriel, who awoke with the sudden alertness of a cat.

'What the hell is going on?'

'There's a tarantula in the bathroom!' They both spoke at the same time but her shriek was definitely a few hundred decibels above his.

'Get up!' Rose demanded frantically. 'You have to go and kill it! Now!'

'You mean before it kills us?'

'It's not funny, Gabriel!' Rose felt close to tears. 'I have a…real fear of spiders.' She imagined it crawling out of the bathroom and scurrying across the wooden floor to her mattress and she broke out in nervous perspiration.

'Okay. You wait here.' He levered himself up, glanced around for something, finally settling for one of the glasses, and disappeared into the bathroom, taking care to close the door behind him.

In his absence, Rose huddled as tightly as she could in her sheet and tried not to think of small, furry creatures finding their way underneath it.

Where was the calm, practical secretary *now?* She groaned to herself. She could barely look at him as he exited the bathroom with a grin on his face. Not that she could actually *see* the grin, but she knew it was there from the lope of his walk.

'Where is it?' Rose asked in a small voice. 'I'm sorry. I'm not being much help so far, am I?'

Gabriel lay down and turned to face her. 'I put it through the window. It was more scared of me than I was of it.' He lightly stroked her hair away from her face and Rose didn't tense up as she normally would have. 'I know you don't like being the damsel in distress, but there's no need to apologise for being afraid of a spider. You're not the exception. Most people are afraid of spiders.'

'Except you.'

'I fear nothing.'

That drew a smile from her, but only for a second, then she sobered up and said quietly, 'But that's not why I'm here. To be a burden that needs looking after—scared of spiders, scared of thunder and lightning. I'm not functioning properly at the moment, I'm afraid.'

'Why is that, I wonder? Maybe you're homesick.' Gabriel had never been so intensely aware of a woman in his life before. If he edged one inch closer to her, he would explode.

'Maybe you're missing what's-his-name…' He realised, with some surprise, that *what's-his-name* had actually been on his mind. 'What *is* his name? Did you ever say? Oh, yes. You did. Joe. Maybe you're missing Joe. Being in love can do strange things to a woman.'

Rose, lulled into a cocoon of security, with the gale force winds gusting outside and the rain as clamorous as hailstones clattering down on a tin roof, was yanked back to reality by the mention of Joe. Joe, whom she had completely forgotten. Joe, perfectly nice and suitable Joe, who was supposed to be her passport to overcoming her feelings for the very inappropriate Gabriel Gessi.

She pulled away, suddenly horrified by her compromising position.

'Can it? Yes, I suppose it can.'

Not the answer Gabriel was hoping for. Not when he was in the process of freely admitting to himself that he wanted this woman, for reasons beyond his comprehension.

'What does that mean?' he found himself asking.

'It means that this conversation is inappropriate.'

'Nothing that's going on here at the moment is *appropriate,* or hadn't you noticed? We're halfway across the world. We're being buffeted by a hurricane outside. We're sharing a mattress on a floor. I'm all but naked and so are you.'

'I…I…'

'Yes?' Gabriel prompted silkily. 'You…what? Want to disagree with something I've said?'

'I don't think we should be having this conversation!' Rose heard the panic in her voice and wondered whether he had detected it as well.

'Why? We *could* talk about work but somehow…I don't think the circumstances are quite right for that.'

'We should go to sleep. Tomorrow will be a long day. Lots to do.'

'I *was* sleeping until you jumped on me.'

'For a reason!'

'But now I'm fully awake and so are you. So let's discuss this sudden love you think you've discovered. I'm curious how it can all happen so quickly.'

'And *I'm* curious as to why you're *curious* in the first place!' Desperation was beginning to lace itself in between the panic but the option of returning to her room was now non existent after the tarantula episode.

'Because it's out of character,' Gabriel told her. 'And anything *that* out of character can't be right.'

'You think you know me, but you don't,' Rose muttered, half truthfully because he sure as heck didn't know how she felt about him.

'You mean you've *always* hopped into bed with men you've only known for a couple of hours?'

'I haven't *hopped into bed* with anybody!' Rose objected and immediately regretted her talent for telling the truth when she saw him smile smugly.

'Now, *that's* more like my Rose.' Some men knew women and Gabriel was one of them. Women loathed being stereotyped. Rose might be sharper, cleverer, funnier and a damn sight more on the ball than the women he had always dated in the past, but she was still a woman. And a woman he wanted. Increasingly. Everything about her had been getting to him recently and lying on a mattress next to her, admittedly under some pretty weird conditions, was not conducive to his attraction abating.

Every primitive instinct in him reared into ferocious life. He had never felt anything like it before. His need to have her, right here and right now, was overwhelming. Accustomed as he was to being in control, the sensation of suddenly being swept along on a roller coaster ride of desire was strangely erotic.

'Because I'm dull?' Rose snapped.

'Anything but.'

'I haven't slept with Joe because we're still in the process of getting to know one another.' She wondered how this situation fitted in with her getting to know another man. And, never mind the situation, how her feelings of suppressed excitement at lying next to Gabriel fitted in with her plans for moving forward with her life, trying on a bit of healthy dating for size. How was she ever going to progress any relationship with a man if her body was still so stubbornly and frantically aware of her boss? How? 'I don't believe in rushing into things. Not if they're to last.'

'And you think what you and some man you've spoken to a couple of times have is *going to last?*'

'Why not?' Rose said defensively. She was finding it impossible to tear her eyes away from him and the soft, lazy drawl of his voice seemed to drown out the chaos of the weather outside. How was that possible? she wondered. And how was it *fair?*

'All relationships have to start *somewhere,*' she whispered. She turned away abruptly and lay on her back, staring upwards at the ceiling. He hadn't laid a finger on her but he might as well have, because her body was responding to his proximity with a mind of its own. Her breasts ached and the moistness between her legs was a shameful reminder of how insanely attracted she was to him. She knew that she was breathing heavily and quickly but she didn't care because it was a feat in itself to have broken the mesmerising spell of his gaze.

'No truer word was ever spoken,' Gabriel murmured.

The soft, feathery touch of his finger on her arm made her swivel to face him.

'What…are you doing?' she croaked.

'Touching you. Do you like it?'

'No.' Rose felt faint.

'Yes, you do.' Gabriel's voice was as soft as silk. 'Every relationship has to start somewhere. You're absolutely right.'

'I don't know what you're talking about, Gabriel.' Her words were punctuated by the sound of the shutters being blown back as the gale force winds ferociously tried to attack the inside of the villa. Gabriel jumped up and even for him it was a struggle to secure them back into place. When he was finished he turned to her, arms folded, and walked towards where she was now half sitting up on the mattress.

'I'm going to check on the rest of the place,' he told her, 'make sure that everything's as secure as it's possible to be.'

'I'll come.'

'No.'

'But…'

'If anything needs securing, you won't be able to help with it. I'm no chauvinist, but even I have to acknowledge that I'm probably going to be better at doing something that requires brute strength.' And besides, he thought to himself, he didn't want her putting on her secretarial hat. He didn't want her sticking on her jeans and gathering herself together. He wanted her warm and wide-eyed and lying next to him. He wanted…

He could feel his body responding to the thought of what he really wanted.

'I'll be half an hour. You stay here.'

Right, Rose thought, as soon as he had left the room. Time for a think. Time to get the brain processes into gear. Put some clothes on. Maybe even drag the mattress back into her room.

She might be scared of errant tarantulas but how much scarier was the thought of Gabriel returning, touching her, talking in that low, husky voice that made minced meat of all her good intentions?

She groaned softly and her hand strayed to where her cotton underwear was mortifyingly damp. Just talking to her—that was all he had done—had left her body throbbing and on fire. One touch there and she knew she would fall helplessly off the edge into mindless orgasm.

No!

Before she could dwell on the heat coursing through her body and on her own craving to have him quench it with his touch, she sprang to her feet and began dragging the mattress towards the door. It was pretty heavy and cumbersome. He had made it seem lightweight when he had dragged it through, but then, as he had said, he was equipped for the heavy duty stuff.

She had her back to the door and was busily trying to get some sort of grip that would turn the unwieldy object into something more manageable, when he spoke and Rose jumped in shock.

'What are you doing?'

Rose blinked in confusion. 'I thought you were going to be gone for at least half an hour? Checking that everything was nailed down?' She was still clutching one tip of the mattress and noticing that he was damp, probably caught out by the rain in one of the rooms. His black hair glistened.

'Everything's nailed down. What are you doing?'

'I'm going back to my room,' Rose mumbled. 'I think it's for the best.'

'Mind if I ask why?'

Rose dropped the mattress and it thudded against the back of her legs, making her stumble. Unless she suddenly developed the secret of body displacement, there was no way she was going to leave the room, not while Gabriel was standing in front of the door, arms folded, as immovable an object as she had ever set eyes on.

'Because the situation seems to be getting a little out of hand.' Rose aimed for her usual crisp voice but it had deserted her. In its place, was something nervous and unsteady and her eyes skittered away from his face.

'I didn't come over here...to...for...' Her words faltered and she cleared her throat. 'The weather's making us both behave out of character and...'

'The weather has nothing to do with it,' Gabriel said dismissively. 'And we're behaving perfectly in character...'

'I don't know what you mean,' Rose said faintly.

'You can scuttle back to your room, Rose. I'm not going to stand in your way, but make no mistake—we want one another. There's no use you pretending that you've got the perfect man in the background. He might be perfect but he's not perfect for *you* or else your whole body wouldn't quiver when I touch you.'

'How dare you?' Rose said weakly. 'That's simply not true...'

'No? Then you wouldn't mind if I put it to the test...'

Rose's mind shrieked a frantic, *Yes, yes I would mind!* But when she opened her mouth, nothing came out. Worse, her eyelids fluttered and, as his mouth touched hers, every bone in her body seemed to turn to water. That probably explained why she found herself leaning against him and why her hands curved upwards around his neck, drawing him down to her as she hungrily, *greedily,* returned his kiss.

Nothing had prepared her for this. That first kiss had been a taster but this was the real thing. He had told her that he wanted her and, just in case she was in any doubt, his kiss was putting paid to that.

His tongue invaded her eager mouth and his hand was on her waist, making sure that she was pressed against him so that she could feel the hardness of his arousal.

Rose whimpered and, when he drew back slightly, she moaned, wanting him back.

'Do you still want to go back to your room?' Gabriel murmured. 'Because, if you do, then tell me now, right now. And I'll take the mattress in for you. But if you stay, then…' He left his sentence unfinished but Rose knew exactly what he meant. If she stayed, then there would be no turning back. They would make love and to hell with what came afterwards, to hell with reality waiting just around the corner. He was giving her the opportunity to change her mind.

'What about…tomorrow…?' She had to ask the question and she didn't mean *tomorrow* in the literal sense. He understood immediately.

'For me, tomorrow is a bridge to cross. But not now. Too much planning for tomorrow dilutes the chance of enjoying today. But that's me. For you…decide now, Rose.'

Rose realised that she knew him too well to escape his meaning. Strip away all the waffle about bridges and enjoying todays…he was telling her to either give in to lust and enjoy the moment because there would be nothing else forthcoming, or else abandon the exercise while he was affording her the chance.

Rose met his eyes steadily and then smiled ruefully. 'But I'll always blame it on the weather,' she murmured before reaching up to touch his face against the palm of her hand.

CHAPTER EIGHT

WORLD WAR THREE could have been happening outside. In terms of the weather, World War Three probably *was* happening outside, but Rose was unaware of it. Gabriel pushed the mattresses back together and then turned to her.

'Don't take anything off. I want to undress you. It's been my fantasy for a while.'

'Has it?' Now *that,* Rose thought, was a truly sexy remark and not one she had ever thought she would hear, least of all from Gabriel, the object of her own fantasies for as long as she could remember.

'Oh, yes,' he murmured. 'You have no idea how erotic some of your buttoned-up suits can be.' He circled her waist with his hands and then, slowly, oh, so slowly, pushed up her T-shirt, savouring every minute of her gradual exposure. First her stomach, silky smooth and flat, then, he drew his breath in swiftly, her breasts, full and perfectly formed with big rosy nipples that begged to be taken into his mouth.

He thought of her, sitting in front of him in his office, legs crossed, notepad on her knee, the epitome of sensible efficiency. When he equated the image with the woman standing in front of him, half naked now as he carelessly tossed the

T-shirt on the ground, groaning as he took her breasts in his hands, he had to will himself to go slowly.

He led her towards the makeshift bed, wishing that he could make love to her in his own king-sized bed in his house. Then he thought that there were lots of other places he would like to have made love to her, not all of them feasible, so a couple of mattresses on the ground was no big deal.

And the storm outside lent a certain something to the ambience.

He got undressed when she was lying on the mattress, gazing up at him. He had never been the sort of man who gloried in his good looks but it was a hell of a turn-on to be performing a strip tease of sorts in front of her.

She was still wearing her panties, white cotton ones. He liked them. In fact, he preferred them to the raunchy, lacy numbers he had encountered in the past, the sort of knickers that left very little, if anything, to the imagination. For the first time ever, he wondered why women seemed to think that obvious won over simple when it came to underwear.

He lowered himself gently on to her. He would take this very slowly. He would savour every leisurely minute of it. And he would start with her mouth, her full, inviting mouth.

Under him, her breasts were soft. He would get there later. The anticipation was excruciating.

Having him lie on her, feeling him hard against her thighs... Rose knew, without a doubt, that she was doing the right thing. At least for the moment. The years, she could now see, had tipped her infatuation into something much, much deeper, and while for him this would only be a physical act, for her it was everything. She moaned softly as his mouth found her neck and he trailed feathery kisses down to her shoulders. When he reached her breasts she squirmed and then sighed blissfully as he began suckling on one aroused nipple, drawing it into his mouth, tasting it the way someone would taste an exquisite morsel of food.

The storm inside her was raging. Even with the savage noise of rain and wind, she could hear herself groaning as she writhed under his exploring mouth.

He was in no hurry. He seemed prepared to linger over her breasts for ever. Rose had always been self-conscious about her body. Her face was average, which was something she could handle, but her breasts were too big. She had been an early developer and had never quite recovered from the shame of being the first in her class to get a chest, and a sizeable one at that. That she had been slim at the time had only made matters worse. So she had put on weight. What couldn't be hidden could at least be camouflaged. Her weight had, in turn, made her self-conscious in front of men and she had never really relaxed or enjoyed sex with the partners she had had, all two of them.

She was making up for lost time. She didn't feel an ounce of shame or modesty as Gabriel continued his attentions to her breasts and when he raised his head and told her that she had the most beautiful breasts he had ever seen, she felt heady with pleasure.

'Fantastic nipples,' he murmured, rising up to kiss her and at the same time pressing himself against her sensitised, swollen clitoris so that she shuddered in swift, immediate response. 'I could lick them for ever. Did you like me doing that?'

Rose nodded and he nuzzled into her ear. 'Then why don't you tell me…?'

'I did. Like it. You know I did.'

'Do I?'

'You should and in case you're in any doubt… I loved you

licking my nipples, teasing them, playing with them with your tongue...'

'Good.'

Rose felt him smile against her neck.

'Now I'll just go and do a bit more exploring before I get you to talk dirty to me again...'

He did. He massaged her breasts, enjoying the weight of them in his hands. Women tended to be too skinny. Rose had lost weight, yes, but she still maintained her curves. There were no ribs showing and she was magnificently well endowed. He hadn't been lying when he had told her that he could spend for ever playing with her breasts. He could.

He nipped the tip of one nipple between his teeth, drawing a pleasingly vocal response from her, and then he felt her gasp as he edged his way lower, circling her belly button with his tongue.

He placed both his hands firmly on her hips and then he was there, breathing in the sweet, musky scent of her womanhood through the cotton briefs.

Rose grasped his hair and tugged him to look at her.

'You can't...'

'Have you never...?'

'I...No...'

'I promise you, I'll do nothing you won't enjoy...' Gabriel focused his mind. He was so close to the edge that he had to physically pause for a few seconds just to get a grip. Never before had he felt so out of control in bed. He gazed up briefly at her. Her back was arched, her head thrown back and her breasts were heaving as though she had run a marathon. He knew exactly how she felt!

She was as close to orgasm. He knew that all he need do was thrust into her and they would both be there. But he wasn't going to do that. Not yet.

He tugged the crotch of the briefs to one side and breathed softly on the fine, downy hair and Rose groaned. When he flicked his tongue along the moistened groove, she wriggled against his hands and then thrust up, offering herself to his eager, questing mouth.

Gabriel tugged down the underwear and it joined the T-shirt somewhere on the ground.

Now they were both naked, flesh against flesh. He parted her legs, hitched them over his shoulders and, amidst the noise of wind and rain, he took her to a place she had never been before.

The sensation of his invading tongue unleashed a wild, unrestrained ecstasy in her. Rose gasped and groaned and she would have come right there against his mouth if he hadn't reared up, sensing the fragility of the moment, and entered her.

Fulfilment was not a long time coming. For either of them. Afterwards, when Rose would normally have felt the need to get back into her clothes, she lay curled into him and sighed. 'Is it my imagination or is the storm beginning to abate?'

'Is that, my darling, all you have to say?'

Did he just call her *my darling?* Was that how he talked to *all* his women after they had finished making love?

'What would you like me to say?' she teased, curling her arms around his neck and sliding against him. Even in the aftermath of their love-making, she could still feel him stir in arousal, and that gave her a delicious, heady sense of power. That she could do that to him!

'You could tell me that the earth moved…'

'No…I don't think it would be morally responsible for me to inflate your ego even more than it already is…'

Gabriel laughed under his breath and brushed her lips with his. 'So tell me now that you're still interested in what's-his-name.'

Rose stilled. 'Is that why...you...because you wanted to prove that I found you more attractive?'

'What sort of man do you think I am?' Gabriel asked. 'I wouldn't be above lecturing to you on your choice of man but I would never sleep with you to prove a point. What I don't want is for you to wake up in the morning and tell me that we have to pretend that none of this happened so that you can pretend to be interested in someone you obviously don't care much about.'

'I do like Joe!' She was, however, finding it difficult to even remember what he looked like. The blond hair and blue eyes which had impressed her because of their boyish charm had been completely obliterated by a man with devilishly dark good looks and a sexy charm that could turn any woman's head.

'But you're not attracted to him. Forget about how *nice* it is to take things slowly. Fast and furious...' he gave her a slow, crooked smile that made her toes curl '...is the mark of physical attraction...'

Rose would dearly have liked to disagree but how could she? 'Fast and furious isn't a good thing all of the time,' she said wistfully. It only worked when it was part of a developing relationship, when the fast and the furious eventually matured into joy and contentment and all the silly little things that Gabriel wanted nothing to do with.

'Helluva lot of fun, though.' Gabriel stroked her thigh and then slipped his hands between her legs so that he could cup her womanhood in a gesture that was almost territorial. And, much as she hated admitting it, very pleasurable.

'And the only reason I want you to admit what you feel for me is because I selfishly want us to carry on enjoying this...'

For how long?

'You're my boss.'

'And so can tell you what to do…hmm…?'

Rose couldn't help herself. She felt her lips twitch. 'Only when it's to do with work,' she said gravely.

'So if I tell you that we're going to make love again…?'

'I might agree or I might not…' But already his fingers were gently exploring her, turning her brain to mush. She closed her eyes and reached down, taking his erection in her hand and sensuously massaging it, then she pressed it against her so that they could be yet more intimate.

'What about if *I* tell *you* that we're going to make love again…?' Rose murmured wickedly. 'Would you be prepared for the shoe to go on the other foot?'

'Absolutely. I'm a feminist. More than prepared to take orders from a woman…'

Later, after a long and lazy bout of love-making, during which they touched and caressed each other everywhere, exploring each other's bodies with the fascination of kids opening presents at Christmas, they fell asleep.

When Rose next stirred and opened her eyes, it was to find that Gabriel was no longer in bed with her and sunlight was doing its best to stream through the wooden shutters that had blown open the night before in the high winds.

Then memories of the night before flooded her mind and she lay back for a few seconds savouring them.

Cold reality, just a heartbeat away, had her dashing to the bathroom so that she could get changed before Gabriel returned from wherever he had gone. They may have made wild, abandoned love but the extraordinary circumstances had disappeared and she didn't want him to return, perhaps regretting his actions of the night before, to find her lying in bed dreamily waiting for him to return.

She realised that she was ravenous, though where they

were going to get food she had no idea. Just as she had no idea what damage had been done to the exterior of the villa, or to the island, for that matter.

She dressed quickly in a small silk skirt, several variations of which she had purchased during her time in Australia. She had brought them with her because they could be rolled into a small ball and unrolled back to their pristine state—and a blue T-shirt. She would have worn slippers but, not knowing what sort of destruction she would find outside, stuck on her flip flops as an afterthought.

The body of the place seemed intact, as she hurriedly left the bedroom and made her way to the front door. Somehow debris had found its way in, but there appeared to be no structural damage. When she ventured out, the scene was slightly different.

Rose stood and gaped. Raging storms were not part of the English weather pattern. She had never witnessed firsthand what destruction their wrath could unleash so it was a shock to look around now and see the uprooted trees, the branches transported and scattered across the lawns, the detritus of building work that had managed to escape its confines and be blown to all four corners. It seemed incredible that the sun was now shining and the sea was blue and calm in the distance. From her vantage point, she couldn't see the beach but she could imagine that it was as littered as the gardens higher up here were.

Then, glancing to her left, she spotted Gabriel, deep in conversation with two local men who were gesticulating and laughing. He wasn't looking in her direction and Rose took a few seconds to appreciate his immense physical appeal. He was wearing a pair of low-slung khaki shorts and an off-white T-shirt with some indecipherable logo on the back. He looked casual, relaxed but, at the same time, totally in command. The two dark men were both shorter than him and were nodding now and pointing. Even from here, Rose could read the deference in their body language.

She took a deep breath and walked over to where they seemed to be inspecting the distant horizon, not forgetting that her role on the island was one of a practical nature, even if last night had blurred it wildly beyond recognition.

She also couldn't allow herself to forget that sex, for Gabriel, was not an indication of anything meaningful, at least not according to *her* definition of meaningful. He might not even want to remember what had occurred between them the night before and, even if he did, he certainly would not expect her attitude towards him to have changed substantially.

Either way, Rose was going to be braced for all eventualities.

Most of all, she was going to be adult about everything. She had slept with her boss and, yes, it had been blistering, but that didn't mean that she would allow it to scramble her brains.

She got closer and hid her growing anxiety under an easy smile.

As soon as Gabriel smiled back, she knew that at least he wasn't going to look at her with disgust at her behaviour the night before and, when he pulled her towards him and slung his arm over her shoulder, Rose tried hard not to read anything into it. This wasn't about love and commitment, it was about a man whose needs had been satisfied and who anticipated further satisfaction of those needs.

She remembered just how blissfully satisfied her own needs had been met and relaxed into his casual embrace. After a while, it seemed natural to be pressed against him and she actually began paying some attention to what was being said.

It seemed that however frightful the destruction appeared to her, the island had actually only received the tail-end of the hurricane. The brunt of it had swung away from the small island, reserving its devastation for American shores. Hence no real loss of buildings and the roads, or rather the one main road and its few tributaries, were intact. Electricity would be back up and running by mid-morning, they were assured, and the clean up programme would only take a couple of days.

It was treated as more of an irritation than anything else. When she worried aloud how the gardens would be cleared of the debris, she was told that it would be taken care of. Most of the workforce would be back by the following morning and they would see to it that everything was sorted.

Wilson, the foreman, was neverendingly optimistic about the timescale involved in the clearing up and even more optimistic about completion of the project. While the boss man was over, he said, they could go through what was left to do, although if he had a look around he would see that there was very little. They could take a boat over to the mainland, choose some of the fixtures and fittings. By Christmas, he told them, everything would be ready. They could come and have a little holiday there, enjoy the sunshine.

Rose thought that by Christmas the chances of them still being together bordered on the unimaginable, although Gabriel, ever diplomatic, was making all the right noises.

By the time they had concluded their conversation with Wilson, Rose was beginning to feel hot. And very hungry. It was nearly eleven. They had not actually got to sleep until the early hours of the morning and she had slept the sleep of the drugged. Heaven only knew what time Gabriel had got up!

'I'm sorry I got up so late,' was the first thing she told him as they headed back towards the villa. 'You should have woken me up.' Just in case he thought that she might want to start taking liberties now that they had slept together.

'You look very sexy,' Gabriel told her, spinning her to face him and pulling her close. 'Did you bring that skirt to turn me on?'

'Of course not!' But she barely had time to protest when his mouth crushed hers and her body reacted automatically. She thought, in a daze of sudden, fierce desire, that it was as if she had now been programmed to respond to him. He kissed her and she kissed him back, hungrily, greedily. His hand grazed her breast, like it was doing now, and her nipples became acutely sensitive, so sensitive that she had to stop herself from pushing his hand under her T-shirt so that he could touch her right here and now, in the middle of the garden and in sight of whoever happened to be around.

'You're wearing a bra,' he murmured into her ear. 'Very bad. In this hot weather, the constriction to the blood circulation could be downright dangerous.'

Rose laughed huskily. 'Would you recommend that I take it off?'

'Without further ado. Right now, in fact.'

Rose went red and looked around her. Daring and sexy was fine in the safety of a dark room at night, but daring and sexy in the middle of the day, in full view of spectators, was a different matter.

'There's no one around,' Gabriel drawled, placing both hands on her bottom and grinding her against him. 'In fact, you could wear your birthday suit here safe in the knowledge that you would be free from prying eyes.'

'What about Wilson and the other chap who was with him?'

'Gone. And because we're on a hill top, we have a commanding view of anyone coming up, not that anyone's likely to. They'll all be too busy cleaning up after the storm. They'll have put their binoculars away for the moment.' He slid his

hands up, under her T-shirt, and efficiently unclasped her bra.
When he saw her shocked expression, he grinned wickedly.
'Not something else you haven't tried, Rose?'

'There isn't much opportunity to strip off in my back
garden,' she told him, 'not unless you want an audience.'

'So you've never made love in a public place?'

'No!'

'Close your eyes.'

'What?'

'Close them and go with the flow…'

She did, helplessly allowing him to pull her T-shirt over her
head, followed by the circulation-constricting bra. The warm
sun felt wonderful against her bare skin, as did Gabriel's
sudden intake of breath as he looked at her abundant breasts.

There were a million things he should be doing. For
starters, he needed to go into the town, find the local bar and
a telephone point so that he could connect to the outside world
and start doing some work. Life in London hadn't ground to
a halt because there had been a spot of bad weather on an
island halfway across the Atlantic.

He also needed to start thinking about doing some basic
clearing up. The workmen would take care of the outside, but
he would have to ascertain what kind of damage had been
done, if any, to the interior of the villa, see what would be
covered by insurance and start working on it.

On the other hand…

He could, as he had advised her to do, go with the flow…

What harm was there in playing truant for a day or two?
When such irresistible delicacies were on offer?

'Of course, if you're going to enjoy the sunshine, you're
going to have to apply some sun cream.' His eyes blazed
across her bare breasts, sending a shudder of electric aware-

ness zinging through her. 'Why don't we have a look around the grounds, just make sure that nothing too immediate needs to be seen to, and then we can take some lunch down to the beach? See what damage has been done there. Hmm?' The irresistible delicacies were too powerful a temptation and Gabriel flicked his thumbs over the pert nipples. Rose felt her breath catch.

'Good idea,' she croaked.

'And I'll take my shirt off as well, to keep you company. Now we'll *both* need to apply the sun cream...'

Rose thought that the trip was developing into some kind of wonderful, surreal experience. Having sun cream smoothed over her bare breasts by Gabriel was beyond even her wildest imaginings, and she had had a few of those over the years. She didn't have an idea where the experience would take her but, for the first time in her life, she was living in the moment and for the moment and relishing every second of it.

They strolled around the grounds, which had been damaged by the high winds, but not substantially so. Gabriel pointed out what would need to be done and filled her in on his plans for the place, pointing out what was intended to go where, asking her what she would choose for this place or that place, seemingly interested in everything she had to say.

Her own private preferences spilled over into her professional advice. How could she remain the consummate secretary when she had slept with her boss and was now walking side by side with him in nothing more than a slip of a skirt? How could she be clipped and businesslike when every so often, as though he couldn't help himself, he would turn to her and kiss her, then touch her breasts, caress them, tease her pouting nipples into peaks? Impossible.

And the scene was almost domestic when they prepared a

light lunch together to take down to the beach. They chatted as though they had known each other for years, as indeed they had, Rose reflected. Four years of picking up all the bits and pieces that comprised someone's personality. They had never shared an intimate moment in all those years, but she still felt as though she knew him intimately and she was surprised how much he knew *her* even though she had never allowed him entry into her private life.

The beach was much as they had both expected. On the walk down, Gabriel pointed his plans for converting the rocky ledge halfway down into a sunbathing patio.

'With the perfect view of calm blue sea,' he said.

'Provided the calm blue sea decides to behave itself.' She had become used to her breasts being bared to the sunshine. It felt wonderfully free. Ahead of her, Gabriel was holding a makeshift box in which they had packed some corned beef sandwiches, some water and a packet of biscuits. It was the best they could rummage up at short notice, not that he seemed to mind. For someone who could afford caviar and champagne on a starched linen cloth with a butler to pour, Gabriel seemed surprisingly happy with the scant offerings from the cupboard.

Rose thought that no picnic could have been better. Even the clutter of branches and coconuts on the beach, not to mention the seaweed and coral that had been dredged up from the storm, was enough to ruin the perfection of the experience.

They had managed to unearth a huge blanket of sorts from a cupboard that contained various assorted items of linen, presumably used by the workmen. To Rose, this was as close to paradise as she could possibly get.

'Now,' Gabriel said, settling down next to her on the blanket, 'I think there's still a spot of sun lotion to be applied considering you'll have to take off that very impractical skirt you're wearing.'

He whipped the sun lotion out of the box and squirted a generous amount on to the palms of his hands. Rose gave herself over to the smell of the salty air, the warmth of the sun and the expertise of Gabriel's hands as he stroked the cream onto her breasts, paying a disproportionate amount of attention to her nipples, which were standing stiff and erect. She felt like a luxuriating cat. Whenever she stirred, he told her to lie back and relax. He needed her, he told her huskily, to remain perfectly still if he was to do a thorough job.

'And close your eyes,' he commanded. His need to possess her, mentally and physically, was overpowering. He worked his way down her stomach, massaging the cream into her skin. She was silky-soft and warm from the sun.

But this time, before he could get her to that mindless point of no return, Rose scrambled up and pushed *him* back on to the blanket.

'*I'm* going to make love to *you* this time,' she told him. 'You'll do everything I tell you to do...and the first thing is to keep absolutely still...so that I can rub this lotion over *every inch of you...*'

Rose thought that she could easily get used to making love in a public place, or at least in a deserted cove on an island in the middle of the blue ocean. With this man. The man she loved and always would love to the ends of the earth.

She didn't want to think beyond the feel of the blanket under her, the sound of the sea, gentle and docile now as it lapped against the sand, the sensation of the salty breeze on their bodies.

If Rose could have captured that moment in a bottle and hung on to it for ever, she would have because she knew that, once it was lost, it was lost for all time. They would never re-capture it again.

And neither could she exist in a bubble, living from one moment to the next.

'…much as I'd like to…' she finished explaining to him. They had just finished having the most amazing sex and a long swim in water that was so transparently blue and calm that it was mind boggling to think of it churning against the rocks the night before. The sun was rapidly drying them. Staring up at the cloudless azure sky, it was hard to believe that she was having this conversation.

Gabriel propped himself up on one elbow and stared down at her, tilting her face so that she couldn't avoid looking at him.

'Who said anything about living in a bubble?' he asked.

'What do you call this…?'

'I call it…my perfect secretary…' He trailed his finger between her breasts, then circled first one nipple, then the other, finally rotating the sensitised nub of each between his fingers. His eyes lazily feasted on her body, the flat planes of her stomach, already turning a pale shade of gold, the V of soft downy hair that shielded her ripe womanhood. The taste of her still lingered in his mouth.

Rose turned on to her side to look at him seriously. 'But it's not reality,' she persisted quietly. 'Reality is London. Reality is me working for you, coming into the office in a suit, sitting at a desk… Reality isn't the two of us on a beach. This is stolen time.'

'It's only stolen if we leave it here,' Gabriel said, bending to place a kiss on the corner of her mouth. It beat the hell out of him how he could have failed to notice just how perfect her lips were. Full and well defined. Like her. 'When we're back in London things can carry on just as they were before…in the office. And just as they are now with you in my bed.'

But she wanted to spend the rest of her life following it through.

The kiss at the side of her mouth deepened into something more urgent, something that sent her body into immediate meltdown. He pulled her close and she rubbed herself against him, head flung back, nostrils flared in pure sensuous pleasure at the abrasive feel of his hard erection against her. When he rammed his thigh between her legs and began pushing against her, she let her thoughts fly from her head.

And that, for Gabriel, was the end of the conversation. It had literally gone from his mind. Rose knew that with unerring instinct and, for a short while, she was prepared to enjoy what was spectacularly on offer. They made love with an intensity and driving passion that was almost uncontrollable. And they overstayed their original four day plan! Rose was amused because, for Gabriel, it was unheard of. One of the bigger islands was a boat trip and short flight away and they made a day of it, buying clothes and various other luxuries not easily found on the small island.

They would stay for a week, Gabriel told her. Things were being accomplished with the villa and, besides, he needed the break. But the week turned into two. They filled the time with trips to other islands, with a bit of work, with lots of love-making. Together they even chose tiles and accessories, which felt treacherously good. At night, wakeful when Gabriel was asleep and still hot with the imprint of his touch on her, Rose lay awake and pondered her options.

Sooner or later, Gabriel would rouse from his unfamiliar slumber and the call to arms would sound its trumpet. He might like the idea of continuing with their loose affair back in London, but Rose had seen too many examples of what happened to the women he slept with once they had outlived their sell-by date. There was no doubt that, sooner or later, and probably sooner, she would end up sending the goodbye flowers to herself.

And Gabriel had no intention of committing to anything other than a fling. He never had and he never would, not until he found the right woman and it certainly wasn't her.

Rose wasn't going to wait until she became an embarrassment. Nor was she going to try and pin him down with questions of permanence. So when, after two weeks, he began making noises about regrettably returning to work, she did the only thing she could think of doing.

She arranged a phone call to herself. It was a little tricky. It involved a call to her neighbour, instructing her to call and to leave an urgent message. Rose would take it from there. Her neighbour was bemused but blessedly tactful and the following lunchtime, hurrying from the public telephone in the town and wearing an anxious expression, Rose told Gabriel that she would have to leave immediately. An emergency. She had run through the various *emergency* options in her head and had settled on one that couldn't be fixed with money.

'A death in the family,' she told him, packing as she spoke so that she wouldn't be able to make eye contact. 'An aunt—' she crossed her fingers '—very sudden. I must go. Mum… Well, they were close, put it like that…'

The clean break she had anticipated when she had returned from Australia was the only option now. If she didn't take it, she knew that at some point she risked her longing and love for him to be transmitted, like osmosis, out of her and into him and her mind shut down when she tried to contemplate the humiliation of that eventuality.

She would see him back in London, she lied, flinging things into her case, knowing that she would get rid of everything, every last memory. Three days—she laughed, half turning to him—not long!

There was a bittersweet poignancy when he held her from behind, when his hand found those places that could send her soul soaring, when later they made love, enjoying each other for what seemed like an eternity.

She wanted to commit every second of it to memory because it would have to last.

CHAPTER NINE

GABRIEL looked at the photographs of the villa that had been scanned and emailed to him. It was virtually complete. Two and a half months ago it had withstood the fury of the weather and it was as if that in itself had been a catalyst for change. Equipment and materials that had been a source of problems, suddenly became available. The workforce had resumed with renewed effort. Everything had dovetailed neatly into place.

He logged off, sending the twenty-two scenic shots back into cyberspace, and pushed himself away from the desk, swivelling his chair around so that he was staring broodingly out of the window at an ever-darkening day.

The sun, the island, the passion, that night of rain and wind and untamed sex, followed by two weeks of the most liberating love-making he had ever experienced, seemed like a dream. *She* seemed like a dream. And not one Gabriel particularly liked springing into his head when he least expected it. Like now.

Three days after she had left, destination one deceased relative, so called, Gabriel had returned to London to find an empty office and a note.

Don't think this is going to work after all. Please don't contact me. I have arranged for a replacement to start work as soon as you return. Rose.

He could recall word for word what she had written because he had kept the note. He wanted it close to him at all times as a reminder of why any sort of emotional involvement with a woman was a mistake and, yes, he *had* become emotionally involved. Not much, of course, but enough. Too much.

He had followed his natural pattern of replacing her with someone else and had been to the right places with the right six-foot leggy blonde clutching his arm and gazing up at him in awestruck adoration but the formula for forgetfulness had failed to work. He had been distracted and unable to find the energy to court her. She, in turn, had been hurt, mortified and ultimately enraged by his apparent slur to her pulling power.

Gabriel had immediately abandoned himself to work. It would have been successful had it not been for moments like…this, when he found himself grimly subjected to the merciless power of memory.

He had no idea why he couldn't rid himself of the inconvenient image of her popping up in his head like a burr, determined to cause maximum irritation. He assumed it was because, for the first time in his life, he had been wrong-footed by a woman. In every single instance he had always been the one who gave the rueful speech about it being time to move on. Now he had been given a taste of his own medicine and he didn't care for it.

Not, of course, that he had any intention of seeking her out and prolonging the debate. That would have been unthinkable.

Gabriel stood up, stretched and loped over to the window. He shoved his hands in his pockets and stared down at the fading day. Curiosity, a visitor he did his utmost to repel, gnawed tenaciously at the back of his mind. *What was she up to? Had she started that course of hers? Was she seeing anyone?* He assumed she would have taken up again with Mr What's-his-name she had left behind. Thinking about that made his teeth clench in anger. *After she had slept with him, proved to them both that Mr What's-his-name was one hundred per cent lacking in the sexual compatibility department, she would go back to the guy just because he represented God knew what...security, he supposed!*

Gabriel glowered through the window at nothing in particular. So far up, everyone and everything looked pleasantly small. He had had nearly three months to mull over her disappearing act and had come to the conclusion that underneath the sexy, responsive woman beat a heart that longed for security. Of course, he should have guessed that she would have eventually been terrified of having an affair with him, terrified of the limitless freedom of expression he offered her. He had allowed the fiery, sexual, hungry side of her to be expressed and she had decided that it was all a little bit too much.

Serve her right if she ended up living a life of drudgery and monotony with a man she clearly didn't love and never would!

Gabriel sat back down at his desk and glared at the computer screen, which obligingly offered him the relaxing vision of company accounts. He lightly tapped one of the keys and the screen shifted to a draft report that needed checking.

It was just as well that she'd vanished if security was the thing she longed for! Because she would know only too well that he was the last man in the world to offer that gem of a prize to any woman. When the time came he would settle down, but that time was still a long way away! The last thing he needed was a messy situation involving someone who worked for him!

He couldn't help but speculate, with satisfaction, that she was probably bitterly regretting her hasty impulse to leave. When she sobered up, it pleased him to think that she would realise just what a financial package she had tossed down the drain. How many companies were prepared to offer an employee a part-time week at an escalated salary, with no guarantee that said employee wouldn't walk straight out of the door the minute they qualified in their studies? Frankly, none, and especially not considering she would be a recent employee at whatever company she had deserted him to join.

No, he was pretty sure that she would be suffering.

Fortified at the thought of that, Gabriel retrieved the photos of the villa and contemplated them in a less aggrieved frame of mind, flicking through them with satisfaction because the place looked stunning even in its as yet unfinished state. Amazing what painting and decorating could achieve! The landscaping, including the golf course, was yet to be completed but that would be the last thing, and the pools, three smaller ones and one large infinity overlooking the sea, were all but up and running.

He wondered whether he would aggressively advertise it as a luxurious, fairly private resort available to a select handful of people who were willing to basically rent an island or whether he would keep this treasure to himself, lend it out to friends, enjoy it with his family whenever he could find the time. His mother was always angling for a family reunion. She could have her reunions in style there.

He was just beginning to pleasantly contemplate the myriad uses to which the villa could be put when he heard his secretary knock tentatively on his door and he bit back the immediate surge of annoyance.

Karen Davis was proving to be an excellent replacement

secretary if efficiency was the only prerequisite. Unfortunately, on most other counts, she didn't press the right buttons for him. She was too young at twenty, too timid and too reluctant to take the initiative. He told himself that he really had to give her time to grow accustomed to his ways but, whenever he thought like that, he began thinking of Rose and then his mind, freed of its leash, would gallop all over the place.

'What?' he snapped, modifying his voice to a more polite, 'Yes?' when Karen poked her head around his door.

She was thin. Some might call it fashionably thin, but to his eyes, she appeared emaciated. Her hair was very long and she was very pale and had a tendency to look away whenever he spoke to her. She *was,* however, extremely good when it came to the basic mechanisms of her job. Gabriel reminded himself of that and of the succession of no hopers he had employed when Rose had gone to Australia. He tried to soften his expression.

'There's someone here to see you, sir…'

Gabriel had tried hard to make her call him by his first name but she persisted in sticking to *sir* and he had given up. 'Who? There's nothing in my diary.'

'No, well, sir…'

'Tell him to book an appointment through you. I won't be working late tonight.'

Karen hesitated and glanced over her shoulder.

Rose, standing by the door, knowing that Gabriel wouldn't be able to actually make her out, sent her a sympathetic glance back. Poor kid. This was probably her first real job, fresh out of secretarial college, all primed on her computer skills but totally green when it came to handling a man like Gabriel. For a few seconds, Rose forgot that she, herself, felt sick to the stomach with nerves. She gently lifted one finger to her mouth, instructing the girl not to pursue the matter and noticed the flash of relief in her eyes.

Karen nodded at Gabriel, who had already lost interest in the identity of his mystery caller, and quietly shut the door.

'You go home,' Rose said gently. 'And I'll go in.'

'But…' Karen looked back at the closed door and chewed nervously on her lip, 'he'll *kill* me if you just walk into his office. Part of my job is to…you know…vet the people who want to see him…'

'Don't worry about it. I'll make sure you survive the ordeal.' Rose smiled, although her mouth hurt from the effort. 'Don't forget I used to work for him. You're not allowing a complete stranger into his hallowed presence…' Rose had met Karen briefly, on the very day she had returned to clear out her desk. Two days before Gabriel returned from the island. She knew that the young girl had been curious about the suddenness of her employment, but she had been easily convinced by the generosity of the pay package. So hers was a familiar face and if Karen suspected that she might not be an entirely welcome visitor—or else why would she have arrived unannounced for a surprise visit?—she was still happy to follow the path of least resistance. Which involved her making a quiet and speedy departure from the office.

With the outside door firmly shut, Rose drew in a deep shaky breath.

She had spent the past four days trying to predict how she would feel standing right here, inside this office. She could have come earlier in the day, but she knew how the office worked, knew that if she timed it well she would arrive when most of the staff were leaving, which would be the better option.

She had anticipated nerves, but nothing could compare to the wild, sick fluttering in her stomach now.

She smoothed her perspiring palms on her skirt and forced herself to walk towards his door. To knock or not to knock? Rose knocked and got exactly what she expected, which was a, *'Yes! What is it now?'* that paid even less lip service to courtesy than when Karen had knocked previously.

She pushed open the connecting door.

Gabriel didn't bother to look up. He was frowning heavily at his computer screen and, for a few seconds, Rose took the opportunity to just look at him.

His masculine beauty, as it always had, jumped out at her, making the breath catch in her throat, although he looked more gaunt than when she had last seen him on that fateful night before she'd walked out of his life. For good. Or so she had planned at the time.

'Gabriel!' Her voice seemed over loud in the confines of the room but it had the desired effect. Gabriel's head shot up and his expression was one of utter shock, very quickly replaced by one of unreadable stillness.

They stared at one another. To Rose, it felt like hours. Her legs felt weaker and weaker but no way was she going to make her way to the chair, that chair facing him that she used to sit on every time she entered his office to take notes. He was the first to break the silence.

'What are you doing here?' Gabriel pushed himself away from his desk so that he could cross his legs and survey the woman standing in front of him, as nervous as a kitten. The fact that he was still raw from thinking about her only a few minutes ago left a bitter taste in his mouth.

Suddenly Rose found that the speech she had rehearsed wouldn't emerge from her dry, stricken throat.

'Sit down. Although I have to tell you…' he glanced at his watch, then back at her face '…I don't have much time to chew the fat with you. I'm out on a date and I don't think the lady in question would appreciate being kept waiting because of some ex-fling.' There was no date in point of fact. He had cancelled the redhead a few days ago, preferring the option of a bit of solitude and the company of his faithful laptop computer but he didn't flinch at lying. He also knew that dismissing her as little more than an ex-fling would cut and, sure enough, he saw her wince, although, to her credit, she didn't take her eyes off his face.

'So. What do you want?'

'I...I...'

'...you were in the area and thought that you'd just pop in and see how I was doing?' Gabriel raised his eyebrows in patent disbelief. 'Now, why do I find that hard to believe?'

'I know you were probably surprised when you got back to London...and found...found that I had left...' This wasn't exactly how she had planned on broaching the conversation, but just looking at him had thrown her off balance.

'Now, what would give you that idea?' Gabriel asked, with blistering sarcasm. 'Is it because, the night before you left, we had made lingering, passionate love? I was obviously deluded into imagining that you might have wanted to prolong our affair.'

'Things change.'

'When did you decide that clearing off was a good idea?' Gabriel found that he was compelled to hear the answers to questions he hadn't even known existed in his head but obviously did. 'Was it when you made it back to the UK?' He digested the barely discernible flicker of hesitation on her face and pounced with deadly accuracy. 'You'd made your mind up *before*, hadn't you...?' Gabriel intoned slowly. She neither denied it nor did she confirm it and her silence was answer in itself. He had been *used*. Gabriel felt as though he had been hit in the gut with a sledgehammer.

'You don't understand, Gabriel…' Rose could feel herself descending into a quagmire of ugly accusations.

'Oh, I understand all right. Shall I tell you how I see things…?'

'No!'

Rose tried to control her shaking hands but she was mesmerised by his cruel, handsome face. She would hear him out. She didn't have much choice anyway because Gabriel, when the mood took him, was an unstoppable force.

'You became my lover because you were frustrated by the boyfriend you left behind here… Don't ask me why—maybe you found that he couldn't satisfy you.'

Rose gaped at him incredulously. She would have burst out laughing if he hadn't been so absorbed in own ridiculous theory.

'And, as fate would have it, we ended up in bed. Although…maybe fate played less of a part than I think. After all, it was *you* who came running into my bed at the first sound of thunder and it was *you* who fled out of the bathroom from a spider, just coincidentally happening to land on top of me…'

'If you recall, I was also the one who told you that I didn't want anything…to happen between us!'

'An impossibility and you knew it!' Gabriel dismissed. 'You must have known that we would have ended up making love. Tell me, did you give your boyfriend the benefit of what you learnt from me?'

Rose clenched her fists tightly. If she had been within hitting distance, she would have struck him across his sexy, sneering face. *How dared he jump to his horrendous conclusions and reduce her in the process?* And why bother to tell him that Joe was no more? The man who'd lasted one date!

It was a joke but she had known, beyond the shadow of a doubt, when she'd returned, that there could be no one for her but Gabriel. At least not for a while. It just wouldn't have been fair to have any man suffer the humiliation of comparison.

'How *could* you think that of me, Gabriel? How could you think that I would be…*calculating* enough to jump into bed with one man just so that I *could practise?*'

'Then when did you make the decision to leave and *why?*' Gabriel loathed himself for his weakness in wanting to know and he gave her a look of cold contempt that she could show up and extract the shameful admission from him.

'I did you a favour, Gabriel.' She looked at him steadily, even though inside she felt as though her nerves were being twisted into knots. 'I knew that you would tire of me sooner or later. I spared you the embarrassment of knowing that you wanted to get rid of me and I spared myself the pain of…'

'The pain of *what?*'

'Never mind. It doesn't matter. It has nothing to do with why I'm here. None of it has.'

In her head she had played around with all the various possible outcomes of her visit. None of them were very comforting.

When he didn't say anything, she frowned and asked unsteadily, 'Don't you want to know why I'm here?'

'I already do.'

Rose's eyes widened. 'You don't! How could you?'

'It's easy.' Gabriel gave an elegant shrug. 'When you cut through all the nonsense, the only thing that speaks volumes is money.'

'But…'

He raised one imperious hand. 'How are you doing on your course?'

'I haven't actually…started it, as a matter of fact. But what does that have to do with anything?'

Gabriel couldn't contain the grim stab of disappointment. Had he really thought her to be any different from the rest of the human race?

'How much?'

'How much what?' Rose asked, dazed.

'How much money are you after to fund your course?' He stood up and strolled over to the window so that he could perch against the ledge and give her the full benefit of his contemptuous stare. 'I wondered how long it would take before you realised just what a good financial deal you gave up here. I guess I could be heartless and tell you to clear off, but hell, what's a bit of money in recognition of your…effort?'

'Forget it, Gabriel.' Rose stood up on trembling legs and turned blindly for the door.

It had been a huge mistake coming here, but she had talked it over with her sister, had seen it as the right and decent thing to do. Now, she could only ask herself what aspect of right and decent Gabriel Gessi would understand when his whole world was ruled by the concept of money.

'Sit back down!' he commanded, but she was already heading for the door.

She didn't get far. In fact, she hadn't even made it to the outer door when he was by her side, spinning her around so that she was forced to look at him.

The touch of his hand on her was like the heat of a branding iron and nor did he release her. He just stared down at her, his fingers digging into her skin, until she finally pulled away.

'I didn't come here to listen to your accusations!' she said in a rush. 'I didn't come here to be accused of being some kind of gold-digger or anything else, for that matter!'

'Oh, why did you come, then? To check and make sure the secretary you procured for me was doing all right? She is. You need have no worries on that front.'

'I came to tell you that I'm pregnant!'

The silence that reverberated around the room was deafening and, for the first time since she had known him, Rose was treated to the one-off sight of her boss rendered utterly speechless. The colour drained from his face and he stared at her for a few seconds, during which she would have sworn that her heart stopped beating.

But he rallied fast. Shock gave way to suspicion. 'That's impossible. We were careful.'

'We were careful most of the time, Gabriel. But we weren't careful on that first night… Do you mind if I sit back down?' If she didn't, she might *fall* down because her legs felt as unsteady as rubber. She sat on the chair and for a while he remained standing behind her, as if locked in one spot. Rose refused to twist around and face him. She couldn't imagine what was going through his head but she was pretty sure that she wouldn't like any of it. Fatherhood was a high price to pay for a couple of weeks of sex with a woman who was destined to be yet another one of his ships that passed in the night. She would never have featured on his agenda at all if she hadn't returned from Australia several pounds lighter, several shades darker and more in keeping with what he considered *attractive!*

She daredn't look at the horror that would be stamped across his beautiful face.

Eventually she heard him walk towards her, past her, towards the window, through which he stared in complete and telling silence.

Most of all, she wanted to tell him that she was sorry but it had never occurred to her, not for a minute, that she would fall pregnant because of a single slip-up. She had stupidly allowed passion to overwhelm the simple matter of taking precautions. Gabriel, mistakenly, had assumed that she was on the pill and the following day, having been assured by her that no, she wasn't protected, but that they had been absolutely safe the night before, he had taken the issue of contraception into his own hands.

She hadn't guessed that, by then, it was too late.

It had taken her sister six months of trying to conceive!

'When did you find out?' Gabriel asked coolly, turning to look at her.

'Ten days ago.' Her eyes fluttered away from his cold, shuttered expression. 'I…I didn't think about my periods until I had to go to the dentist and she asked whether I could possibly be pregnant because I needed an x-ray to be done. Then it occurred to me that I hadn't had one for ages.' She knew that her words were tripping over one another but that look in his eyes…

When she had rehearsed what she would say, the scene had never unfolded in her head like this. Yes, she had anticipated being nervous, but she had her speech all down pat. She was pregnant. She took full responsibility for what had happened. She felt it only right that he should be aware of the situation but she wasn't about to impose on him, either emotionally or financially. In her head she emerged from the messy situation as proudly independent, open and willing to negotiate whatever visiting rights he might want, but also open and willing to accept that he might want very little. After all, a child had never been part of his game plan and she should know because, in a weird way, she knew him like the back of her hand.

'What makes you think that I believe you?' Gabriel asked.

Rose looked at him, startled out of her gut-wrenching apprehension. 'What do you mean?'

'I *mean*,' he said, his tone of voice implying that what he was about to say would be logical beyond all dispute, 'I suddenly discover that you find me irresistible. You've worked for me for years and yet, five seconds after arriving on the island, I've suddenly turned into the man of your dreams. Odd, wouldn't you say?'

To refute this sweeping, inaccurate observation would have left her wide open and vulnerable, so Rose remained silent, waiting for him to develop what he meant.

'Particularly odd,' Gabriel continued, 'considering you'd just got yourself a boyfriend...' He thought of the way she had run out on him and his fiercely wounded male pride was like the sharp edge of a knife, goading him into accusations which her changing expression was making a nonsense of. He couldn't help himself. He particularly couldn't help himself when he thought about what's-his-name and the possibility that she might, actually, be seeing him again, sleeping with him. Who was to say differently?

'Now you swan in here, months after you've walked out on your job, with some story about being pregnant.' His mouth twisted into a cynical sneer. 'If you *are,* and I'm not even willing to admit to that, who's to say that you weren't already pregnant when you came with me on that trip? Who's to say that your sudden, overwhelming need to hop in the sack with me wasn't a ruse for you and your lover to con me out of money?'

Rose's shock showed in her white, disbelieving face, sufficient for Gabriel to feel a morsel of guilt at his casual shredding of her character.

She made to stand but he was in front of her before she was halfway to her feet and she fell back into the chair, wincing away from his dark, oppressive anger as he leant over her, his arms on either side of the chair like steel bars.

'Don't even think about it!' he grated. 'Don't even think that you can come in here and tell me that you're pregnant with my child and then leave!'

'And don't *you* think that you can accuse me of being a gold-digger or of *using you!* That's the most insulting thing anyone has ever told me! *How dare you think that I had some kind of ulterior motive for sleeping with you?* It says a lot about you, Gabriel Gessi, that you could have such a...*vile* opinion of another human being!'

Gabriel shot to his feet and walked away, hands shoved deep in his pockets. He raked his fingers through his hair and swung round to look at her.

'What can you expect?' he muttered. 'You've come in here with a bomb and detonated it at my desk.'

'I'm sorry.' An icy calm had settled over her. Yes, he would be in shock, but his extreme reaction was somehow easier to bear than if he had offered help or compassion or even money. She wasn't even sure why she was so surprised and wounded at his raw accusations. Gabriel was filthy rich and he had the instinctively suspicious mind of someone who *was* filthy rich. And she could concede—just—that pregnancy was the fastest way to a man's wallet. The hurtful part wasn't his cold, detached approach to what she had said, it was that he had thought it in the first place, that he had allowed his flawed intellect to take precedence over what he must surely know about her by now.

'I know you're in a state of shock,' she said tonelessly. 'I debated whether I should come and tell you or not but in the end I felt you should know. And, before you leap in with any more accusations, let me tell you straight away that I'm not after your money. This wasn't part of some elaborate plot to rip you off. I can't go back in time and take back

what happened between us on that island but I didn't
connive for it to happen.' She risked a glance at him and felt
a sharp stab of compassion. 'And it's yours, Gabriel. I
haven't seen Joe since I got back to England and, anyway,
I never slept with him.'

She suddenly felt desperately weary. The past ten days
had been a struggle. In fact, the past two and a half months
had been a struggle. She had returned to London, jobless, and
had immediately found herself a decent enough temp job.
But it was uninspiring and left her ample time to mourn what
she had abandoned. She was tormented by the thought that
she should have stayed, had the affair he had offered, waited
to see what happened. She had salvaged her pride, saved
herself the eventual let-down, but her bed was cold and lonely
at night and her mind chattered ceaselessly with argument and
counter-argument.

She had also dropped her plans to go on her business
course. Somehow she didn't feel herself to be in a positive
enough frame of mind.

So she had drifted miserably from one day to the next until,
ten days ago, when two bright blue lines on a home pregnancy
testing kit had galvanised her out of her depressed torpor.

Now here she was, having done the right thing, facing
down a barrage of accusations. She gritted her teeth against
the desire to cry.

'Okay, let's just say I believe you...' He did. The truth was
written all over her face. Nor had he really believed for a
second that she would have wilfully slept with him so that she
could later spring a pregnancy tale of woe on his shoulders.
Nor did he know what had compelled him to lay into her with
such force. But he believed her. She was carrying his baby.

Gabriel, who had never once contemplated the reality of

fatherhood except as some distant situation that might or might not arise in the fullness of time, was shocked to realise that his initial feelings were ones of pure, virile satisfaction.

He felt as though he had *triumphed*.

'Yes…?' Rose was treading warily.

'Which isn't to say,' he added, 'that I won't demand a DNA test somewhere along the line…' He wouldn't.

'I'm not lying to you, Gabriel. Would you believe me any quicker if I told you that I didn't come here today to try and get money out of you? That I came because I thought it was the right, moral thing to do?'

'You must know that there's no way I would let any son of mine go without…'

'*Son?* Hang on a minute…'

'Or daughter, of course.' He gave an elegant shrug and then began prowling the room, forcing her to turn around to keep up with his progress. 'Whatever. No child of mine will be allowed to go without.'

'Naturally it will be up to you, whatever you decide to contribute to his or her welfare.'

'*Contribute?*' He gave a bark of laughter and paused to look at her with incredulity. '*Contribute?* You speak as though my own flesh and blood would be on the receiving end of the occasional donation! No, my involvement will be *much* more far reaching than a cheque sent out once a month…'

For the first time since she had disappeared, Gabriel felt the angry restlessness inside him begin to ebb away as he contemplated, with calm acceptance, a future he had not banked on.

'What do you have in mind?' Rose asked, her voice even more guarded.

'Put it this way, Rose…' He sat behind his desk and looked at her. Yes, he could see now that she had put on a bit of weight. Not so much that you would notice, but enough. She looked glowing. 'No child of mine will be a bastard.'

'Meaning…?'

'Meaning that you'll have to marry me.'

Rose gazed at him, shocked by his Draconian solution. 'I don't intend to do any such thing!' she informed him adamantly. 'We're no longer in the Dark Ages, Gabriel. Children are born out of wedlock all the time. There's no longer any social stigma associated with that.'

'Irrelevant.'

'No, it's not *irrelevant!*' Marry him? Live a life knowing that he had tied himself to her because of a child? Was there a faster way for a marriage to turn sour between two people? 'I can't marry you because I'm pregnant!' Rose struggled to make him see her point of view, aware that she was battling against the traditionalist core of a dinosaur. 'It's the worst idea I've ever heard. You didn't *ask* for this situation!'

'That I won't deny…' So why, he wondered, didn't he feel worse about it?

'And I'm sorry but I won't let you bury yourself in matrimony with me because you feel obliged…'

'I don't think I mentioned that you had a choice.'

Rose thought about marriage and her expectations of it. None of them included her loving a man, having his baby, desperately waiting and hoping that one day he would return her love. Nor had she ever looked forward to the inevitability of a husband who would stray because he would eventually become bored with her, bored by the sight of her. A child was many things but superglue wasn't one of them and a marriage artificially sustained because of one would be a marriage made in hell.

'You will marry me, Rose. It can be a small affair or you can lay on all the trimmings, but marry me you will.'

CHAPTER TEN

GABRIEL, in what was becoming a familiar situation of disgruntled uncertainty, clicked off his mobile with a frown.

He was sure that there had been a man's voice in the background. Or maybe it was his imagination playing tricks on him. It had been doing that lately. Ever since he had found himself on the receiving end of Rose's determination.

No marriage.

Naturally, he had assumed, with his boundless self-assurance, that he could steamroller over her objections, and he had given it a damn good shot.

For every point she raised he had countered it with ten of his own.

To claims that he was behaving like a Victorian tyrant, he had pointed out that his intention was merely to honour his responsibilities and ensure that his progeny was born with the greatest advantages of having a mother and father, both living under the same roof, both sharing the decision making.

'You will never be able to accuse me of not doing the right thing,' he had told her with pride.

And, just in case she remained unconvinced, which she surely couldn't be, given the indisputable logic of his arguments, he had ticked off, on his fingers, every reason for marrying him.

The benefit of security for his son. Or daughter, he had hastened to add. The benefit to *her* because she would be financially secure, able to fully appreciate motherhood without feeling the need to go out to work. Additionally, he had told her, they got along and were attracted to one another. It was hardly as if they were sworn enemies being forced into an unnatural alliance!

To any further obstacles and to reassure any misplaced sense of pride, he had informed her that she could look on it as something of a sensible business arrangement.

'As you do?' she had asked blandly, and he had nodded thinking that, yes, it really *was* something that made sense. And, to top it off, it made him *feel good.* He had never thought that the prospect of marriage would make him *feel good.* Rather, he had always privately maintained that, whatever tales he had heard to the contrary, most men, himself included, would view the institution of marriage as a regrettable cessation of the sheer joy of the affair, the vigour and excitement of the chase.

But, surprisingly, he had felt nothing like that and he could only assume that the prospect of fatherhood was more powerful than he had ever imagined.

So it had come as a brutal shock when she had stuck to her guns. No marriage.

Threats to drag her up the aisle had met with stony silence and he had resorted to dangling all manner of financial carrots in front of her, at which point she had turned her back on him and thrown over her shoulder that, unless he stopped pestering her, not only would she not marry him but she would find it hard to have *anything* to do with him at all!

Pestering her! Just the memory of those two words made Gabriel's teeth snap together in baffled fury.

He was certainly left in no doubt that the last thing she was was a gold-digger! In fact, he sometimes caught himself half wishing that she was more impressed by his wealth. At least then he might have been able to pin her down!

As it was, she was now in her sixth month of pregnancy and there was still no prospect of any ring going anywhere near her finger.

Gabriel had even consulted his mother on the best way of tying her down, expecting keen support from that area—after all he came from a family of traditionalists—but he had been woefully let down. His mother had quizzed him, asked all the right questions, sympathised with his dilemma which, as he pointed out, was the irrational dilemma of a man thwarted from doing the right thing, and then confounded him by saying that he couldn't make someone do something they didn't want to do.

He had been reduced to *visiting her,* as often as he could, and he had arranged his work life to fit in accordingly.

He said nothing when she told him that there was no need and, over time, she had stopped telling him. Of course, he didn't like the fact that she was still working but, when he'd mentioned that she had laughed and told him that pregnancy wasn't an illness, that it was a perfectly natural condition and putting her feet up would only make her put on too much weight.

However, he was reassured that she had postponed the business course, which would have been sheer lunacy.

Apart from the marriage issue, which appeared to be going nowhere fast, things seemed to be progressing nicely and privately Gabriel had been working on a plan to buy them a house. He would let her choose it. Would let her fall in love with it. And then, maybe, he could entice her into doing what he realised he wanted more and more.

Now this.

Had he heard a man's voice in the background? It occurred to him that she had seemed a bit breathless down the phone.

It was nine-thirty at night! Why would she be breathless? Gabriel, on the way to the airport, tapped on the partition separating him from his driver and gave him immediate instructions to turn around.

He wasn't turning around *to check up on her,* he told himself. Naturally there was no man in the house! Why should there be? She was six months pregnant with his child! And over the months he had come to appreciate that she was not deceptive by nature. She could no more lie to him than she could flap her arms and fly to the moon.

On the other hand, it wasn't as though they were married, was it? She had maintained her freedom even if he was convinced that she had no intention of using it. Damn it, they were still making love! He had done his homework. Read the pregnancy books. Was convinced that sex in the latter stages of pregnancy was absolutely fine, provided there were no contra-indications.

For a few seconds, Gabriel's mind drifted to the eminently pleasing recollection of their passionate love-making. He wasn't ashamed of admitting that her ripe body was a massive turn-on for him. Her breasts were now more than a generous handful and her nipples had swelled and darkened and seemed to have become ultra-sensitive, judging from the way she squirmed whenever he licked their stiffened peaks.

He shifted as his body responded swiftly and inevitably to the mental pictures in his head and he told the driver, in a clipped voice, to hurry.

If she sounded breathless, he decided, then he had to check it out. Purely on health grounds. His deal halfway across the world would just have to wait. He phoned his secretary, utterly unapologetic about disturbing whatever she happened to be doing, and told her to cancel all arrangements for him for the next couple of days. Thrown in at the deep end, she had certainly smartened up her act over the months. He still had to spell certain things out for her and she would never attain the level of responsibility that Rose had, but she would know what to do in this event.

That dealt with, Gabriel stared through the window as the car tackled London on a dark, dank, wintry Thursday night.

His thoughts were all over the place. Right there and then he made the decision that he would not leave her place until he had persuaded her to move in with him. Okay, she hadn't yet agreed to marriage, despite his reasonable approach, an approach that made sense from whichever angle it was viewed, but they would live together. Not ideal, but that way he could keep an eye on her.

The journey took thirty-five torturous minutes and, as the chauffeur-driven Jaguar pulled up to the kerb outside her house, Gabriel was witness to the one thing he didn't want to see.

The male voice in the background hadn't been a figment of his over-active imagination after all. It had been all too real and Gabriel didn't need to look very hard to know the identity of the mystery guest. Who else could it be but the ex-boyfriend?

He sat in silence for a few seconds, clenching and unclenching his fist, watching the man sling on his coat even as he walked down the road away from the Jaguar, reminding himself that he had no control, ultimately, over what she chose to do with her life.

He was overcome with a feeling of failure, an emptiness that was quite unlike how he was used to feeling.

He rubbed his eyes with his thumbs, clearing his head,

trying to silence the roar in there, then he told his driver that he could head back.

'I'll make my own way home,' Gabriel said tersely, pushing open the car door. Jealousy was threatening to overcome every shred of self-control he possessed. He made it to her front door before she even had time to hit the staircase.

Rose heard the banging and immediately assumed that Joe had left something behind.

She wasn't prepared to find Gabriel standing outside her door. Not that it wasn't a wonderful surprise. It was. Because she had thought that he would be at Heathrow, waiting for his plane, although in truth her mind wasn't as sharp as it had been before she became pregnant. She smiled and waited for his responding smile but none was forthcoming. Instead he stepped wordlessly into the hall and turned around to face her.

'What are you doing here?' Rose asked, hesitating at the expression on his face. 'I thought you were on your way to Hong Kong...'

'It would seem that there was a change of plan.' His instinct was to lay into her with questions about what the hell that man was doing in her house, but he restrained himself. Over the past few months, he had discovered a reservoir of patience he had never known existed in him and he called upon it now. Arguing would be no good for her in her condition and, besides, it occurred to him, he seldom won.

A change of plan and so he'd rushed over to her house. Rose tried not to feel flattered but she was. The man who had never actively pursued any woman was pursuing her now and it took all her strength to remind herself of the reason for that. The baby. Had it not been for the baby, she would no longer have been a part of his life. He hadn't bothered to search her out when he had returned from the island and found that she had left his company, after all. And his marriage proposal. That, too, was all about the baby and she respected him for his alacrity in accepting responsibility, but he was no closer to seeing now than he had been months ago that a loveless union was worse than no union at all and he didn't love her. He was willing to take care of her because she would be the mother of his child and he was, as he had pointed out in various ways, an Italian traditionalist through and through. But not once had he mentioned love.

Rose could see all the advantages in marrying him. He would be a generous husband and a fantastic father, but she knew him well. Playing the dutiful husband to a woman he didn't love would grind him down and, over time, inevitably, his eyes would begin to wander. And, looking the way he did, it would be all too easy for temptation to meet opportunity.

There was no such thing as guaranteed fidelity within a marriage but, as far as Rose was concerned, most marriages at least started out with the expectation. For her, it would be like waiting for an axe to fall and there was no way she was going to do that.

But it was hard. When they made love, the feeling of total completeness was as uplifting as it was painful.

'What was the change of plan?' Rose asked, leading him towards the sitting room. Too much standing about tired her out these days.

Normally, he would sit next to her on the squashy sofa, but this time he settled for the chair by the fire.

'We need to regulate this situation,' Gabriel said abruptly. He had waited for her to raise the subject of the man leaving the house, but she hadn't. She obviously thought that they would have missed each other by a few minutes and he was damned if *he* was going to ask questions. He felt sick with rage and jealousy.

'Regulate...?' Rose was baffled by the statement. She yawned and was startled when he asked her, rather coldly, if she would mind staying up so that she could listen to what he had to say.

'What's the matter?' Rose asked, suddenly sitting up. 'What's wrong? Is it work?'

'Work couldn't be better,' Gabriel said icily. 'And if I appear to be in a bad mood it's because I am angry with myself for allowing this situation to go as far as it has done. It is no longer satisfactory for us to be living apart. In three months time you will give birth to our child and I don't intend to remain an occasional visitor to your house.' Nor, he thought savagely, do I intend to let other men have contact with my child!

'But, Gabriel, we've talked about this!'

'And, like a fool, I have indulged your crazy desire to maintain your freedom!'

'It's got nothing to do with *maintaining my freedom!*' Rose told him painfully. 'What exactly do you think I'm going to with this so called freedom I'm desperate to maintain? When I'm at home with a baby?'

Gabriel ignored that. He couldn't think straight. In his mind, the only thing he could see was that man leaving the house. He burned to lay into her, demand to know what the hell she was playing at, inviting strange men into her house, and he loathed his own weakness in feeling so desperate.

'Good. Then we compromise. And I really don't care if you refuse, Rose, because I will simply stay put until you agree.'

'What's brought on this change of mood?'

'A clear head,' Gabriel snapped. 'You don't want to marry me. Fine. You're right. I cannot drag you kicking and screaming up the aisle, although how your conscience allows you to jeopardise the stability of our child's future is beyond me.'

'I don't know h…'

Gabriel raised one imperious hand to silence her protest. 'But there is a limit to what I will tolerate. If you won't marry me, then you will live with me.'

'Be your mistress?'

'Call it whatever you like. The description is immaterial.' He gave one of those nonchalant shrugs of his although his eyes remained very firmly focused on her dazed face.

'I don't see the point,' Rose muttered, but she was exhausted by his drip, drip technique. He had used a sledgehammer to crack a nut but once he had clocked into the fact that she wasn't budging, Gabriel had changed his techniques and over the months had become the master of subtlety, making small but consistent measures to chip away at her resolve. Sometimes she had the unsettling suspicion that part of his persistence came from the fact that she presented a challenge he felt compelled to overcome. It was a disturbing thought.

'What was the urgency to rush over here at this hour to discuss this?' she asked, stifling a yawn. 'I'm really tired.'

'I'll bet.'

Something in Gabriel's voice made Rose stiffen. Now she knew that something was wrong. 'What does that mean?'

'What do you *think* it means?' Gabriel threw out belligerently.

'I have no idea. Are you going to tell me or are you going to try and make me guess?'

'Who was he?' Gabriel heard himself ask the question and it was as if his vocal cords were functioning without the agreement of his brain, because he certainly hadn't intended to reduce himself by asking.

'Who was *who?* What are you talking about?'

'Don't give me that *butter wouldn't melt in your mouth* act! I wasn't born yesterday, Rose!' He sprang to his feet and began pacing the room, releasing some of the high voltage energy that was threatening to make him really explode with her. He daredn't look at her bewildered expression when it must be obvious to her exactly what he was talking about. I mean, he thought savagely, how many men did she entertain when he wasn't around?

Now frankly disturbed, Rose padded across to where he was standing by the window, arms folded, his eyes aggressive slits. She placed her hand worriedly on his arm and he shrugged it off.

'I have *no idea what you're on about.*'

'There was a man leaving this house when I drove up,' Gabriel said, struggling to maintain his composure. 'Why do you think I flew over here? What do you imagine I meant when I told you that my plans had changed? I heard his voice in the background when I spoke to you earlier on the phone and, sure enough, I get here and what do I find? A man leaving this house. Cool as a cucumber! And you acting as though nothing's happened! Well, it won't do! You're going to move in with me and that's the end of it!'

'Are you *jealous,* Gabriel?' Rose couldn't squash an excited flutter of hope. If he was *jealous,* surely that meant that he felt more for her than lust, which would pass, and a sense of duty?

'Should I be? I come here, I see a strange man leaving your house late at night… Tell me, *should I be?* Furthermore, I notice you still haven't told me who the hell he is! No need. I can guess! What's-his-name off the business course! Am I right?' He looked away from her and tried not to imagine the worst. Somewhere inside, he knew that his fears were groundless but, like a leaf caught up in a storm, he was incapable of anchoring himself. 'I hadn't realised that you two were still in contact.'

'We're not.'

'No? The figure leaving the house was really just a figment of my imagination?'

'Joe's called me a couple of times…'

'Joe's called you a couple of times…'

'Well, yes.' Now she felt guilty that she hadn't mentioned the calls. Partly her lapses in memory were to blame and also the fact that she had known that Gabriel's reaction would probably not have been too understanding. She hadn't reckoned on it being as extreme as it was, however, and guilt brought a tinge of colour to her cheeks. Gabriel was on to that in a flash.

'But I don't know what you're so worried about. I mean, there's no need for you to be jealous…' Rose laughed self-consciously and, in some corner of her mind, she was aware that this time Gabriel had not denied that he was jealous. 'Look at me, Gabriel and tell me what you see!' With her smock dress and thick, forgiving cardigan, she was like a ship in full sail.

'A very sexy woman…' Gabriel affirmed through gritted teeth.

Something in Rose melted. She walked over to her handbag, which was on the chair, and rummaged inside, finally extracting a piece of white card which she handed in silence to him. Gabriel glanced at it, then read it.

'He's invited *us* to his engagement party,' Rose said. 'He phoned a few weeks ago because he's a nice guy and he wanted to find out how I was doing with the pregnancy. He mentioned that he'd met a woman and things were serious. I was pleased for him.'

Gabriel stared down at the invitation. He should have been alarmed at his huge overreaction but he wasn't because he knew why he had reacted the way he had. Why he was so desperate to marry her, why, when faced with her constant refusal, he was now desperate to have her live with him. The writing on the card looked blurry and he realised that he was no longer focusing on it but travelling down the blindingly obvious paths his mind was revealing to him.

He looked at her and cupped her amused, gently quizzical face in his hands.

'Okay. Here's the deal,' he said sombrely. 'You have to move in with me because it's driving me nuts living apart from you.'

'What are you saying?' Rose wanted to hold her breath, close her eyes and wish as hard as she could that he would say what she wanted to hear, but reality never worked that way, so she held his gaze steadily and waited.

'I'm saying...' Gabriel ran his fingers through his hair and fidgeted. Finally he led her to the sofa and tugged her down to sit next to him, close enough for him to still touch her face. 'I'm saying...that I can't think straight with you living on your own here. I've felt it for a while but I denied it. Now, I *know*.' He sighed and looked as if he might be trying to put his thoughts into some kind of coherent order. 'Seeing that man leaving here...imagining...well, I can't tell you...seems crazy but that's what you do to me. You make me crazy.' He kissed her gently on the mouth but pulled back before they could find themselves unable to break apart. He needed to talk without the distractions of her amazing body. But, as if he was still compelled to have some level of physical contact with her, he placed his hand on her stomach and she, in turn, placed her hand on his.

'I can't concentrate properly. I worry about you.' He

looked at her carefully. 'I thought I wanted to marry you for the sake of the baby,' Gabriel told her. 'But somewhere along the line things have changed... No...things had changed *before* then. Sometimes I wonder whether what I felt for you was there all along, from way back when, just something waiting to be revealed...'

'*What you felt for me?* What do you feel for me...?'

'I need you...' Gabriel felt as though he was falling off the side of a precipice. 'I'm in love with you...'

Rose looked at him and smiled, a slow, mesmerised smile that only touched the depth of her happiness. 'Will you marry me?' she asked. 'Because I'm in love with you too and you have no idea... I've been waiting so long for you to tell me that you love me too... I never dared hope...' The baby kicked and they both looked down.

'My darling,' Gabriel murmured, marvelling at how his frantic life suddenly made sense, 'I'm yours for ever...'

MILLS & BOON®   0207/01b

Live the emotion

Modern
romance™

THE SPANIARD'S MARRIAGE DEMAND
by Maggie Cox

Leandro Reyes could have any girl he wanted. Only in
the cold light of morning did Isabella realise she was just
another notch on his bed-post. But their passion had a
consequence Leandro couldn't ignore. His solution: to
demand Isabella marry him!

THE PRINCE'S CONVENIENT BRIDE
by Robyn Donald

Prince Marco Considine knows he's met his match when
he sees model Jacoba Sinclair. But Jacoba has a secret:
she's Illyrian, like Prince Marco, a fact that could endanger
her life. Marco seizes the opportunity to protect her...by
announcing their engagement!

ONE-NIGHT BABY *by Susan Stephens*

Five years ago, virginal Kate Mulhoon met top Hollywood
producer Santino Rossi – but he knew nothing of her
innocence, or of the baby they made that one night
together... Now Santino is determined to find out what
Kate's hiding, and once he does he *will* make her his...

THE RICH MAN'S RELUCTANT MISTRESS
by Margaret Mayo

Interior decorator Lucinda Oliver's latest client is
gorgeous playboy Zane Alexander. Lucinda's determined
not to be one of his conquests... But when their work
takes them to the Caribbean, she's seduced by the exotic
surroundings – and Zane's sizzling desire...

On sale 2nd March 2007

Available at WHSmith, Tesco, ASDA, and all good bookshops
www.millsandboon.co.uk

FREE

4 BOOKS AND A SURPRISE GIFT!

We would like to take this opportunity to thank you for reading this Mills & Boon® book by offering you the chance to take FOUR more specially selected titles from the Modern Romance™ series absolutely FREE! We're also making this offer to introduce you to the benefits of the Mills & Boon® Reader Service™—

- ★ **FREE home delivery**
- ★ **FREE gifts and competitions**
- ★ **FREE monthly Newsletter**
- ★ **Books available before they're in the shops**
- ★ **Exclusive Reader Service offers**

Accepting these FREE books and gift places you under no obligation to buy; you may cancel at any time, even after receiving your free shipment. Simply complete your details below and return the entire page to the address below. You don't even need a stamp!

YES! Please send me 4 free Modern Romance books and a surprise gift. I understand that unless you hear from me, I will receive 6 superb new titles every month for just £2.80 each, postage and packing free. I am under no obligation to purchase any books and may cancel my subscription at any time. The free books and gift will be mine to keep in any case.

P7ZEE

Ms/Mrs/Miss/Mr...Initials ....
                                                                    BLOCK CAPITALS PLEASE

Surname ....

Address ....

....

....Postcode ....

Send this whole page to:
The Reader Service, FREEPOST CN81, Croydon, CR9 3WZ